NASTY NEIGHBOURS

This is a work of fiction. Names, characters, business, events and incidents are figments of the authors imagination. Any resemblance to actual persons, living or dead, or actual events is purely coincidental.

Prologue

Daisy buried her head in her husband's chest and sobbed. She was not sure how much more she could take. How could people be so despicable? How could their life have spiralled into such a nightmare that they had to endure this Daily stress? Surely things could not get worse than the deliberate vandalism of their car, the latest in a litany of hateful incidents that were to continue as their enemies increased the pressure to force them out.

Frank held his protective arm tightly around her shoulder and tried to reassure her that everything would be alright in the end. All they needed was to be left alone to enjoy a peaceful retirement. As he spoke, the feeling of rage and helplessness burned inside him. He thought back to the idyllic life they had left behind only a year ago and remembered the old adage that you don't know what you have until it's gone.

Chapter one

Shall we retire?

Daisy Best was sitting in her lovely, sun filled garden room that years before, Frank had converted from part of the old honey-stone milking parlour. He had gone to pour them both a *sundowner* in the farmhouse kitchen. Returning with two glasses of ice-cold white wine, he joined her in the oak and glass garden room to watch the sun set in the distance. It was their favourite part of the whole farm.

The old milking parlour had been built two hundred years earlier, on the edge of the farm's orchard. They did not know which had been there first but the sun's rays would cut though underneath the old apple trees as it went down like a burnt orange. They loved that spot, but this evening was different. As they sipped the wine, their chatter turned to retirement.

They had been on the farm for many years and had brought up their children, two sons: Sam and Ben and their daughter, Louise, there. It held so many happy memories, many of which, came flooding back to them as they contemplated the future.

Nestling in the heart of The Cotswolds, the farm had always been a busy place. From the farmhouse kitchen window, one could see the cattle chewing contentedly as they moved across the beautiful lush green fields, or the horses, running down from the paddocks to the five-bar gate, whenever they saw Daisy, hoping for a carrot treat.

There were the hens that provided eggs for them and their guests, popping up everywhere, while local villagers dropped in to buy eggs, filling their own boxes. It was a warm, hearty place, the most wonderful cooking smells escaping from the kitchen, where life ticked along, everyone enjoying the moment as they passed through the bucolic life.

Throughout the autumn season, the local hunt would ride across their farmland; horns a-blowing, smart red jackets, and the gentleman in oh-so-tight, jodhpurs. 'Tally ho!' It was a quintessentially English country sight: the horse jumping stone walls with varying degrees of success according to the skills of the riders, splashing through streams, usually in the opposite direction to the Wily fox who had more intelligence and cunning than they credited him.

During the run up to Christmas, many of their neighbours and friends would come by to collect the turkeys they had ordered the month before and share a glass of mulled wine and a mince pie. While they were there, most of them would chop themselves a Christmas tree to take home. Frank had planted them every autumn for twenty-five years; rows of trees, glistening with frost early in the winter mornings or shining a bright green when the brilliant winter sun broke through, touching the sparkling dew with brilliant light. The trees created a real winter scene and added to a time of year that they both particularly enjoyed, every year there were plenty for everyone. Frank just enjoyed seeing the fruits of his labour providing more habitat for wildlife. He never a made a profit from the modest charge he made for each tree taken away.

The bed and breakfast guests who stayed in luxury rooms in the converted stone barns, loved it all, the whole package; many of them booking their next stay before they checked out from their present vacation. To visitors from London, especially, it was "The Good Life" and "Darling buds of May" rolled into one.

The icing on this idyllic cake for Frank and Daisy was that they were blessed with wonderful neighbours: Ruby and Hugh, who had lived next door to the farmhouse for ever. Every so often, they would come round and the four of them would while away the evening in the garden room with a bottle or two of wine.

Ruby didn't walk so well and no longer drove a car, so Daisy used to take her shopping in town every week to get her supplies. She regularly made a fish pie for the elderly couple who had no family nearby, their children having moved to different corners of the country. Frank was happy to cut the grass for them as Hugh was not much fitter than Ruby but the old couple still sowed their vegetable plot each springtime and always shared the copious fruit and vegetables that they produced. It was a part of the life they enjoyed together with their neighbours. Frank was always smiling when he returned from a visit next door with arms full of beans, carrots or whatever was in season at the time. Life was definitely good.

    The Bests' children had flown the nest long ago to build their own lives and were now raising their own children. The farm's herdsman had just retired and so the cattle were going, Daisy continued with the bed and breakfast in the barns which Frank had lovingly restored and converted to four star accommodation but every day they met with guests from all over the world and now it was time that they saw that world themselves.

    As the sun slowly disappeared behind the distant hills, Daisy and Frank finally both agreed what each of them had known for some time; the house was too big for them. They had worked hard all their adult life and it was time for a change. Clinking their glasses in salute to each other, they finished the wine and resolved to get the farm valued the next day. Following that, they were going to look forward to the next part of their lives together, whatever that may be.

    They could never have imagined how this perfect life would be ruined in the space of a year. Petty jealousy and gossip stemming from one person would pit their new neighbours against them, turning their retirement into a living hell.

Selling up

Tuesday morning arrived, a gloriously perfect summer day. Frank was up early, thinking about the decision that had been agreed the evening before. Was it the right one? Daisy was in the kitchen, fixing breakfast for him: Tea, toast and kippers, his favourite, 'After all, this is going to be a big day and you'll need some energy!' She had joked. She had every faith in her husband to make the sensible choice.

Leaving Frank to enjoy his kippers, she went out to open up the hen house. She prided herself on having the best kept, most spoiled, chickens anywhere. These were truly free range and every evening she went through same rigmarole of rounding up the last one or two stragglers before shutting them in at night aware of the resident fox who was never far away. As she raised the door, the hens flooded out, some pecking around her feet as if in greeting, while others ran flapping their wings in the sudden brightness of the day. It was a little pleasure that she felt sure could be replaced by something else once they had left the farm.

On the way back to the farmhouse, Daisy checked on the baby apples in the ancient orchard, it was going to be good crop. The huge, gnarled old trees produced many different types of old-fashioned apples which Frank especially, loved but as for the names of each variety… they didn't have a clue. They tasted great and to them, that was all that mattered. She would make apple sauce from the fallers and freeze it down to accompany roast pork dinners in the depth of winter when it would remind them of late summer sunshine. There were far too many apples for the two of them so at the farm entrance every autumn, sat a big box full accompanied by a sign proclaiming: "FREE APPLES – HELP YOURSELF".

As she entered the kitchen, Frank was stood leaning on a worktop, looking ever so slightly apprehensive. "Well I phoned the estate agent; he will be coming out at two this afternoon. I didn't actually expect an appointment so soon."

Daisy busied herself tidying the kitchen for the visit. She felt excited and nervous; what would they do and where would they go on the next part of life's great adventure?

In the event that they should sell the farm quickly, Frank had a plan in mind. "Christmas Cottage" was the middle one of a terrace of three pretty little stone cottages in a nearby village, the other two being "Ebeneezer Cottage" and "Pudding Cottage". No one knew who had named the cottages in the dim and distant past but it was the cutest row. The Bests owned "Christmas Cottage" which they rented out as a holiday home to tourists. It was to be a nice little pension going forward for the soon to be retired couple.

Christmas Cottage was just big enough for them to squeeze into with their clutter and various treasured collections for the time it took to find their new home. Everything else could all go into storage with the farmhouse furniture for the duration. The only problem he could foresee was that they didn't know what they were looking for.

Frank assured his wife that the right property would show itself, although first, they needed to sell the farm. But what was there not to love about it? He was confident that the first people to view it would fall in love and buy it just as he and Daisy had done years before.

Lunch was enjoyed, the dishes washed and just as the kettle was boiling for a cup of tea, the farm gate bell rang. Daisy's heart leapt, It was him; the estate agent had arrived.

As soon as you say the word 'farm', when arranging an *appraisal* by an estate agent, You can be sure of a visit from the senior partner who will invariably be sporting a wax jacket and armed with a pair of green wellington boots 'Just in case'. They will arrive in a four-wheel drive vehicle of some description and greet you in an imperious manner, generally with a mouth full of plums. They are definitely a stereotype and they come up with a big price if you're a buyer. *Yet smaller if you are the seller? Odd that.* Daisy thought.

There was nobody more ordinary than the Bests but they weren't phased by the realtor. They were still a good-looking couple; Daisy was always well dressed and wore her make-up and hair well. She had modelled in her younger days but by the time she reached twenty it was over; she wasn't tall enough. Her best friend who was six inches taller, had gone on to model for Ralph Lauren. They remained friends, but different heights! Frank was just the loveliest man, always ready to help anybody in need and generous to a fault. Everyone loved him. As a couple, they just worked hard and cared about those around them. Everyone in the village had a good word for them and they would be genuinely missed.

The estate agent began his appraisal of the property: 'Umm, six bedrooms, two converted barns and twenty acres.' He read from his notes in a languid drawl. There was also an old cottage in the grounds, where in years gone by, the herdsman had lived but now, much improved, it housed family guests or friends.

'What a lovely old orchard.' he commented. The old apple trees stood proudly in their beautifully architectural shapes with the sun dappling the neat grass beneath them. 'Stunning view.' How could he not be impressed? 'And a stable block...' As he came to Daisy's pride and joy, he could not help but be impressed. 'Oh! 'What a beautiful garden room.' He exclaimed.

'Yes.' said Daisy. 'And we have a sunset.' She couldn't help adding. It sometimes felt as if that sun belonged to her and her husband. The view was part of their life.

After lots of 'ooh's' and more than one 'ah', he completed his professional tour of the buildings. As they all trooped back into the kitchen, he jotted some calculations and gave his estimate of the farm's value. The sellers gave him what they hoped was a non-committal reply: 'Oh, oh. Okay.' but inside they both thought it was just what they wanted. They were thrilled. This would make buying somewhere to retire easier and of course, they also wanted to help their children. It was all going to work out well.

'And', said the estate agent, 'I have a lady who is a professional home searcher for clients nearby. They are a young couple with three small children.' he offered. 'I told her about your property before I came out here, she is keen to look at it tomorrow if that's alright with you. If she thinks it fits the bill, she'll come back later in the evening with her clients for a viewing.

Wow! How could they take all this in? It sounded too good to be true. Neither of them had expected things to move this quickly but then it was a rare property.

The next morning arrived and so did the lovely lady home searcher. Her name was Claire and very efficient she was. She had a good look round and said that she thought it would suit her clients; they had horses for their children as had Daisy and Frank all those years ago. it was time for the next generation to do what they themselves had done with Sam, Ben and Louise.

Sam and Ben now knew that their parents wanted to sell up. Louise was away working so the news would keep. The boys were happy, it had all become a lot of work for their parents They had built a successful business and now it was time to slow down.

Claire returned later that day with her clients, lovely, polite people who the vendors took an instant liking to. They had lots of questions: 'Will you be leaving these beautiful curtains? How old is the heating system? Do you have gas? How far is the nearest pub? how long do the Christmas trees grow for before you cut them? Do chickens bite?'

It was a very funny exchange of questions and answers. A final question and a most important question: 'What are the neighbours like?'

'Oh, Ruby and Hugh are our lovely neighbours, they're the best you could have.' Daisy gladly informed them. 'They are a really lovely, genuine, kind couple. They are getting on in years and we help them out where we can. Oh, we are good at adopting nice people.' She added with a chuckle.

'We will look out for them and take over where you leave off.' Replied the husband of the would-be buyers. *Sounds like he's already decided to buy!* Frank thought to himself.

Daisy and Frank had spent many an evening with Ruby and Hugh. Despite the age gap, the two couples got on like a house on fire. They would sit and listen with delight to stories of the old couple's early life in Kenya where Hugh had worked for the Government. They had been friends of Sir Wilfred Thesiger, the great explorer and travel writer and when Hugh began to talk it was like being transported to Africa; the stories of wild nights, wild animals and wild drinking under the African sun and its enchanting starlit nights. The stories were endless. They had obviously had the most amazing romantic young life together on that exciting continent. Daisy was sure they would get on with this young family next door.

Meanwhile, the young couple excused themselves to wander off and take another look around as their three little girls chased the chickens. it was beautiful, just what they wanted and more. They marvelled at all the Christmas trees, it was so magical, all they had ever dreamed of. They walked through the paddocks, past the chickens and through the orchard, looking back at their children enjoying the openness of the farm.

Once left alone with Frank, Daisy made a tray of tea and put it in the garden room. As the potential farm buyers returned from their exploring, she was waiting: 'Would you like a cup of tea?' the young family came in and sat down, grateful for the refreshment and the chance to chat some more with the vendors. 'Look.' said Claire, 'The sun is going down. It's just like a burnt orange.'

Frank smiled and squeezed Daisy's hand and led her back to the kitchen. There was silence between them, neither needed to say anything.

The quiet was broken by Claire's jolly voice as she let herself back into the farmhouse. 'They love it. They say it has a lovely feel and it would make a perfect family home for them. They'll discuss it together tonight and ring me in the morning. But I think it really is as good as sold.' Wow! this was almost moving too fast. *She's a buying agent, she surely shouldn't be telling us this.* But Claire was as captivated by the farm as her clients were.

Chapter two

Leaving

Saying goodbye to friends and neighbours is never easy. it's like leaving a job, you can't face the boss. Change is difficult for most people; it's just the way life is. Daisy and Frank had become great friends with Ruby and Hugh over the years and now they needed to tell them about the sooner than expected, sale of the farm.

Frank arranged with Hugh to meet for lunch at the pub in the village the following day. The four of them sat at a window table and chose from the traditional *pub grub* menu.

While they waited for the food to arrive, Frank broke the news to their friends. They were more than a little sad but understood that the farm was large and that their neighbours were just getting older like themselves. He and Daisy reassured them that the likely new owners of the farm were absolutely delightful and they were certain they would get along nicely with them.

The landlady came bustling over: 'Fish and chips for the ladies. I'll be back with the steak and ale pies.' As she returned with lunch for the men, she said: 'Well I hear you're moving. We will miss you both so much, it just won't be the same. Make sure you come and visit won't you.' Daisy and the pub landlady had a good arrangement. Her bed and breakfast guests used the local pub for their evening meal and if anyone asked at the pub for accommodation, they were directed to the farm for accommodation. The guests bought newspapers and bits and pieces from the local shop in the village, so it all worked nicely and for everyone there was harmony and mutual respect.

'Go on, follow your dreams.' she said told them. 'I really hope you find a lovely home to settle, somewhere near your children.'

The farm was in the heart of a vibrant tourist area and the bed and breakfast brought valuable revenue to it. Daisy had enjoyed her part in creating the tourism in their village. When the farm had been split up and sold off for housing and the land divided, she and Frank had bought what was left, with the idea of converting the barns for holiday accommodation. It had worked better than they could have imagined and the village was alive again. She felt justifiably proud of her contribution, now it was time for something new.

The paperwork for the sale of the farm was moving swiftly along. The Bests were busy packing, chasing memories in the drawers of the old farm dresser, trying to decide what to take with them and what to put in storage. They were slowly moving things over to Christmas cottage in preparation for completion day.

The night before they left, Daisy was sat in the garden room, the sun was getting ready for bed. She felt a silent tear drop from her cheek and quickly sniffed as she saw Frank coming.

'Darling,' he said 'tonight we toast the sunset. I promise it will follow us, Daisy.' as he passed her a glass of perfectly chilled champagne.

The day came when a team of four cheery removal men arrived bright and early. Despite drinking enough tea to 'sink the navy', according to Daisy who was manning the kettle all morning, the men had their two brightly painted pantechnicons, loaded by mid-afternoon. The lorries pulled out of the driveway taking a lifetime's possessions to the storage facility: there was no chance of everything fitting into Christmas Cottage.

That's it, all loaded and ready for the next adventure in our lives. They both took one last look back at the farm as they pulled away, completing the little convoy of vehicles. *Funny.* Daisy thought. There would be so many things to miss: The bin-man that came every week, who was so helpful and the lovely postman who would always hide the post in the log store when they were away on holiday. Trusty people in your life that we all take for granted until they are no longer there. It was a strange feeling, now everything would be new, building friendships and finding those people again.

Pulling up outside Christmas cottage, they were both full of excitement. The pretty little row of stone cottages covered in pink roses looked as if it had come straight from an old-fashioned chocolate box. They knew the neighbours well and everyone was expecting them. The neighbours from one side, Janice and Steve, invited them to leave the chaos of packing boxes and join them for supper of lovely shepherd's pie, so kind. Knowing this, Jim and Jane on the other side of the cottage, brought the wine, so there were six for supper. The newly retired farmers felt at home.

Looking for a new home

Ever Since the young couple had looked at the farm, even before they made their offer to buy it, Frank had been searching for a new, smaller home. They wanted to be close to the family, have at least two bedrooms, a big garage for him, plenty of parking and a garden.

The housing market had been quiet, not many properties seemed to be available, everything that came up for sale was just not right. Meanwhile, the neighbours at Christmas cottage, Janice and Steve, had become grandparents and their daughter lived in Australia so they decided to emigrate to be nearer to her. Frank and Daisy were sorry to see them go but it presented them with a no brainer opportunity, and they bought "Pudding Cottage" from them. So now they had "Christmas" and "Pudding" cottages. "Christmas Pudding", it made everyone smile!

So the guests that had been coming to them over the years at the bed and breakfast could now stay in the little "Pudding Cottage" and be self-catering. It would continue to give them a valuable income for the future. Everything was coming up roses.

It was a Friday morning and Frank couldn't put off getting his haircut any longer. 'I'll drop the car off for its service and walk down to the Barber's.'

Having left the car, he had a couple of hours to kill so there was no hurry. He paused to check an estate agents window, *just in case*. As he scanned the advertisements, he spotted the manager of the agency gesticulating to him from behind his desk. Frank went in and greeted Adam, whose father had also been an estate agent and a good friend of his.

'We've got a cottage coming on that might interest you if you're in the market for one.' Frank assured him that he most definitely was in the market for a cottage and would consider anything that he could work with. Adam only had very sketchy details about the property available so far but it sounded as if it had potential. He assured Frank that if he could call by on Monday afternoon, he should have a lot more information about the property. The only thing he knew for certain was the name of the village where the cottage was. 'It's in a little place called Whisperswood, about twenty miles up the road.' Frank knew of the village and his mind was racing while he sat through his haircut. He had already decided that he and Daisy would be taking a ride out there on Saturday.

Chapter three

Whisperswood

Arriving in Whisperswood, Frank and Daisy found a small village. Most of the houses were built around the traditional village pond, an eclectic mix of mismatched stone, half-timbered or brick, side by side in short rows. In the corner was the village pub; "The Duke's Head"; all white painted plaster and dark oak, joined to a cute little village store. More houses were dotted along the lane that ran out from the centre. The pretty cottages reflected in the still black water of the pond, from where a solitary duck quacked at them in expectation of bread. It was only a couple of miles from their children, one of the main boxes ticked. This was looking good.

They parked the car on the roadside, in a convenient space by the pond and walked. It was a picturesque place, quintessentially English so they followed the narrow road around the village pond that lead to an ancient looking bridge over a river and continued with pretty stone houses dotted along a leafy lane. All the houses had delightful front gardens, most of them boasting pretty roses, the branches heavy with blooms. This looked like a nice, peaceful place to settle.

Just on the bend of the lane, to one side, there was a beautiful, large old house, very grand looking but sadly overgrown and with an air of not being loved anymore.

Opposite it on the other side of the lane stood another of just the same attractive architectural design but smaller and greatly neglected. It was hard to see very far into the property for the dense, overgrown greenery. At the front there was a small enclosed garden complete with broken picket fence and overgrown hedgerow. To the side was a beautiful but also overgrown, holly hedge that must have been there many years. The house looked empty and was certainly in a very sorry state. Maybe this was the house for sale? There wasn't much to see without climbing through the brambles and they could not really do that until they knew for sure that it was the right house.

They sauntered back to the car, admiring the tranquil setting. 'There's nothing we can do now until Monday when I talk to Adam.' Frank started the car and they set off for home. As they drove through it, they could see that the village was shaped like a giant soup spoon: the large village pond then the lane that narrowed and became leafier as it rose up a gentle hill, the long elegant handle.

Chestnut Cottage

Adam received the keys to Chestnut Cottage late on Monday morning and the first thing he did was phone Frank with the news. It was, indeed, the neglected cottage that they had looked at on Friday. Adam was busily rearranging his diary so that he could accompany them over for a viewing later in the day. 'It's called "Chestnut Cottage", Frank. How do you fancy that?' He added with a laugh.

Daisy and Frank had jumped at Adam's invitation and that afternoon they were outside Chestnut Cottage early. They pulled into a car-sized opening in the overgrown holly hedge that led onto a rutted parking place and waited for Adam to arrive. They just had time to walk along the front of the house, before he drew up behind them, bumping up onto the verge to park. Adam was always immaculately dressed, a good-looking young man with "estate agent" written all over him. He tiptoed off the long grass trying to keep his shoes clean, and bounded up to Frank and Daisy, shaking hands with each of them.

'Great to see you both again.' He beamed. 'I haven't been inside yet so I can't say what we'll find. It was always a rental and as you can see, the tenants are long gone. Even so, it doesn't look like they were gardeners, does it?' He laughed again. Adam found humour in most things, he was just one of those people who are always happy.

As the three of them picked their way along the broken, overgrown path to the front door, the potential buyers asked the first and most important question of the agent: 'What sort of village is it Adam, friendly?'

'It seems quiet.' Adam replied, somewhat guardedly. There had been two houses for sale in the past couple of years. The latest one, just down from Chestnut Cottage, had been sold and he confessed that he had had problems with the woman buying it: 'A snooty, know-it-all type. She threatened to have me sacked, thought I was incompetent.' Another laugh. 'She was just not getting her own way and phoned the office screaming and shouting.' His boss had dealt with her, in the end. Adam was a well-respected and much liked man, locally so to have someone like this, cast aspersions on his character, was particularly upsetting for him. Frank glanced at Daisy as they heard this. She caught his eye and they both knew what the other was thinking: *We have always had good neighbours, they are one of the most important things.*

'They live down towards the village pond, not really near "Chestnuts".' remarked Adam, sensing the vibe. 'You should be safe.' he laughed.

So Whisperswood was a small village and hopefully friendly. They wanted it to be a nice place as the cottage was already captivating them. Daisy and Frank were not the sort of couple to be in and out of other people's houses but would rather pass the time of day and greet their neighbours whilst out and about. True they had enjoyed more than the odd glass of wine in the garden room with Ruby and Hugh, but they had been special friends. They figured they would be okay, though. They had lots of family nearby and as Daisy had grown up not far away, she had many friends. This, they thought could be made perfect.

Standing at the front door as he tried the lock with various keys from a small bunch, Adam started his agent's commentary: 'Here we are then, ready to put your own stamp on it: Detached two up two down, lots of out buildings. That's if you can find them, ha ha!' He hesitated, 'Actually, it looks like rain, shall we look outside first? Come though the garden.'

As they entered the garden a very old woman came marching over, stomping through the brambles as if they did not exist. At first, they thought it was a man, possibly a tramp but it was just that she was dressed in men's clothes, very odd and unkempt, with large clumpy men's shoes lacking laces, that were too big for her. She peered through large, bottle-end spectacles, a man's tweed cap crowning a shock of unkempt white hair completed her unconventional appearance and a large booming 'Do you know who I am?' voice announced her arrival.

'Who are you?' She demanded. This was a woman who would never need a megaphone! Adam recovered from his surprise and politely introduced himself: 'This house is for sale and I'm the estate agent. I'm just taking a couple of viewers round it.'

'Are you nice people?' she barked at Frank, ignoring Adam completely and before anybody could reply she continued: 'if you're not, bugger off!' With a contemptuous wave of her hand, she did an about turn and marched off out of sight behind the greenery.

all three of them were horrified at the outburst from the apparition but after exchanging shocked glances they kind of guessed and agreed that she was just a nut case from somewhere as she disappeared. A gut feeling of warning flashed though the would-be purchasers, but both chose to ignore it, enchanted as they were, with the prospect of a new home that looked as if it would tick most boxes required.

The house was more neglected than it had at first seemed. The garden was a scruffy field with large trees and brambles that stopped anyone from exploring very thoroughly. It had always been the cottage for the cook at the large stately home whose estate the village had been part of and it had gone with the job. Adam had a thick folder containing all sorts of paperwork relating to the property which he kept referring to, in order to impart little snippets of information to his clients.

    The oldest papers showed that the cook had run the kitchen for the Duke, whilst her husband, amongst other things, had made split chestnut stave fences for the estate in years gone by. Split chestnut fencing is simply rows of slim wooden staves held between twisted lengths of wire top and bottom: a cheap and quick solution for penning in the many sheep reared on the estate. In those days it was a constant need on the land. So it was that the cottage had become "Chestnut Cottage", locally, known, simply as "Chestnuts". It had never been sold before as it had always been one of many tenanted houses in the village, owned by the Duke. Some still had staff living in them who worked loyally for him. He was grand man and very well liked. The main house where the Duke lived was a fabulous Georgian pile. With the tenant at "Chestnuts" now retired, the decision had been taken to sell the little cottage. The Duke's main business had shifted from country farmer to country park with walks open to the public, he just didn't need as many staff as his father had before him.

    The garden at "Chestnuts" was very large, just how large, they couldn't tell but only a small patch was accessible due to the overgrowth. It had clearly not been gardened for years and was just the sort of challenge that Daisy excelled in. All sorts of junk was laying half buried in the weeds, from broken bicycles to an old pram to an antique railway porter's trolley! At least two tumbled down wooden sheds were just visible beneath the vines and brambles but it would take a lot of hard work before anyone would know what was actually there.

    Following Adam into the house, most people would have been horrified at what they saw but to Frank's eye, with his years of experience of buying old properties, the neglect and dereliction was all potential. There was nothing in the house that could be salvaged or used. Under layers of badly hung wallpaper, the old lime plaster was falling off. The woodwork was hidden beneath a hundred years of thick, cheap paint and the windows were so rotten, they looked as if they would let everything through except the daylight!

Frank and Daisy loved it. it was the right location, so close to their children. They could always change the house but as the cliché goes: Location is everything and there was plenty of land for any changes they decided upon. They definitely needed a large garage as a priority.

Adam was visibly disappointed at the state of the house inside, he had been hoping that it would be better than the exterior. He cheered up when Frank told him that they would definitely be interested in making an offer for the sorry looking place. Adam knew that he was a man of his word and agreed to wait for a phone call from him with the offer later that day, after he had given it some thought.

They returned to Christmas Cottage, feeling optimistic and in the time it took to drink a cup of tea, they had agreed on a fair price to offer for 'Chestnut Cottage'. It only took two short phone calls to Adam and the offer was accepted. The Duke just wanted rid of the property quickly, with no delays, to a buyer with cash and a good track record.

Moving on

Now that the problem of finding a permanent base was solved, Frank and Daisy planned to take a holiday whilst the bureaucracy of the property purchase ground its way towards completion.

Having had many guests at the bed and breakfast over the years they were not short of friends to visit in nice places. They started by flying to the south of France for three weeks, to stay in an apartment they had bought many years before. It would be a great base to see friends and revisit old acquaintances that had been neglected due to the pressures that go with work and bringing up a family.

In the south of France, the sun would be shining, with the heat of the daytime cooling just enough to give pleasant, warm nights.

It would be a very welcome break. They both loved long walks on the beach and through the bustling streets with the little cafes on every corner exuding the wonderful Garlic smells of lunches to come.

There was one lovely walk in particular that they always enjoyed with Daisy's old school friend, Johnny. He played saxophone in the local jazz bars and was a great showman. Naturally, he was the most amazing company, a "happy chappy" who was always fun: 'Let's eat! Let's drink! Let's party!' He always got them the best seats wherever he was playing, and they had had some wild nights with him. It was he, who first showed them this great walk. They would take the train from Nice along the most wonderfully scenic, coastline-hugging ride to Monaco. Alighting from the train at the village of Eze-Sur-Mer they would then take a slow walk back to Nice along the beach, using the little pedestrian pathways.

They never grew tired of the whoosh of heat that hit them when the train door opened at the little station. Wow! it was always such a beautiful day. They set off walking along the most amazing beaches, until they arrived at the lovely restaurant, "The African Queen", to take a light lunch, including a glass of chilled rose, of course.

Walking on, round the beautiful coves, stopping at more tiny cafes where they could sit a while to soak up the warm sun and enjoy the atmosphere, taking in the wonderful view of the beautiful azure water of the riviera. Finally arriving back in Nice before sundown, to rest tired feet and get ready for Dinner later in the evening. This was heaven to Frank and Daisy; the contrast of the peaceful coastal paths and the busy city all in one day but always the Mediterranean warmth.

Johnny had an apartment in the building next door to their own. While their apartment faced the sea, Johnny's overlooked the street but on the roof of his top floor apartment, he had a swimming pool overlooking the Promenade Des Anglaise. The three of them spent many an evening on the roof, often with Johnny's latest belle making up a foursome, enjoying each other's company, chatting, sharing stories and always laughing. Daisy always brought the nibbles and chilled wine and they sat, toes in the pool, watching the sun disappear over the horizon. It was as if there was a gap between the edge of the sea and the bottom of the sky. Pop it was gone. A wonderful sight to watch. 'Look Daisy, the sun's going down. That sun follows us everywhere.'

Johnny would say: 'Telling our stories is how we organise our lives together in the spaces we live, and this space is small.' It seems amazing that so many people lived in these apartment blocks overlooking the sea and they all rubbed along nicely, bumping into each other in lifts and on the stairs: 'Bonjour Monsieur, Damme.' They would greet the English interlopers and be on their way.

Returning refreshed, from France, Mr. and Mrs. Best went on to sign the first stage of the paperwork for the purchase of "Chestnuts" and waited for completion on the deal to happen. They were getting impatient to be moving to Whisperswood, now that the day was drawing closer. Meanwhile, whilst waiting, Frank contacted his architect to draw plans to redesign the house and talk ideas over.

The grandchildren were so excited that Grandma and Grandad would be nearby soon. They would see much more of each other and that meant more sweets and treats. There would be so much exploring for them to do in the huge jungle garden.

Since they had arrived back home, the weather had still not warmed up, even though it was now July, so when they got their first sunny day, Frank went out to spend the morning in his garage tinkering with his beloved collection of vintage motorbikes. He had ridden since he was sixteen, both his uncles had been Isle of Man TT riders, as had his brother and father, it was in the blood.

Frank had been involved in an accident years before in which he had lost an eye and now the other eye was giving him trouble so these days, he was confined to tinkering instead of riding. He was able to undertake engineering work and made many parts for the vintage motorcycle owners and enthusiasts, he was always busy. Frank was a man's man. He could turn his hand to anything and would never say 'no' to a job if someone needed his help, always happy to take a request to produce parts that had long ceased to be made. He was doing his best but his eyesight was becoming more of a problem; he would trip over steps and stand on Daisy's toes. She didn't mind, she loved her Mister Best and was heartbroken over his loss of sight.

Finally, the purchase of Chestnut Cottage was completed and a mad few days of hard work with the help of some good friends, saw two rooms and the tiny kitchen, cleaned spotlessly, ready to make a start on the rest of the house.

The week before they moved to Whisperswood, Frank had to have surgery on his eye so most of the packing and organising was left to Daisy. She booked the removal men while Jim and Terry, two of Frank's good friends, moved his bikes to their own garages whilst the couple settled into their new home and made space for them.

Chapter four

Moving in

Moving day arrived. This would be a home to retire to, conveniently near the family, all of whom were very excited. Their sons helped with putting things in the right rooms for their parents and Louise made them a beautiful picnic of all their favourites: fresh salad, chopped with Italian ham and a little mustard, as well as yummy little cupcakes that she had made for the occasion. She had packed everything required for making tea and coffee, plus a nice bottle of wine. It was all going to be great.

Daisy was in the bramble-infested front garden of "Chestnuts", even worse now, with overgrown roses from the last season and broken picket fence now collapsing, overgrown privet hedge hanging over into the lane. She was looking out for the removal lorry, to point him in the right direction, when a young woman came almost literally bouncing up; a skinny girl with wild hair who Daisy could not help but notice, had an unfortunately large, crooked nose, perhaps it had been broken in the past. she was dressed in an oversized wax cotton coat and an "awfully terribly" matching wax hat with a band of tweed round it. To complete the picture, she was wearing riding boots and hanging onto the, de-rigueur, Labrador, which was straining on its lead, panting, with its tongue hanging out.

'Well.' She gushed. 'Are you the new people?'
Congratulations, Sherlock. Daisy thought.
'Yes.' She kept the uncharitable thought to herself.

'Well actually, tonight I am having a dinner party. You see, I have a new kitchen, oak! and I am going to show it off to the ladies of Whisperswood from 7 o'clock.'

'That is very kind but I really won't make it.' Daisy replied, apologetically. 'I don't even know where my clothes are!' *and besides,* she thought, she wouldn't leave Frank; he was still recovering from his operation.'

'Oh! well we would really like you to come.' *We?*

'As I said, I really will not make it but thank you for asking.' The woman with the big nose didn't like the refusal and seemed a bit confused as to what she should say next. But surely, she didn't really think that Daisy could manage to go? She was in the middle of moving house, after all!

'Have you met Joan yet?' she blurted out. 'She's always up and down with the dogs. I'm quite friendly with her. She's lovely, she drinks a fair bit, likes a bit of gin… quite a lot, actually. People will tell you she shoplifts at the supermarket, she used to pinch bottles of gin. Quite amusing really, I wouldn't have the nerve, but she hasn't done it for a long time…I think. She's coming tonight, you will meet her.'

'That's a real shame but like I say, I am really sorry but I simply won't be able to make it.'

'Oh well, if you can, we're just up the road there.' She was pointing into the distance. Daisy wasn't sure if the woman was pointing out a specific building, but she had little interest in looking. The only thing she wanted to see was her removal lorry.

The big nosed woman dragged the Labrador through a 180 degree turn and trooped off in the direction she had just pointed in, the dog pulling her along behind it. It had been a strange encounter.

I wonder who Joan is? Daisy was still looking out for the removal men, when another lady appeared, jeans and jumper, trainers on her feet. *Ah, there is normality here*, carrying a big, square Tupperware box. 'Hello.' she said. 'I saw you arriving, so I have baked you a cake.' She had a kind face and seemed a good soul. She introduced herself as…Daisy didn't catch her name; she was too shocked at the size of the cake!

The lady welcomed her and her family to the village and, breathlessly explained that she lived just a few doors down. She apologised that she could not stop as she had a busy day ahead and with a little wave, she was gone. Now Daisy was beginning to think that everyone must be behind their curtains, watching the new neighbours arriving. *how?* she thought, *how could you bake a cake so quickly?*

Fortunately, she spotted the removal lorry before anyone else could waylay her. She waved them down and showed them the nearest place to park up. As the same cheery removal men who had emptied the farmhouse, climbed out of the cab and started opening up the side and rear doors of the lorry, she lifted the cake box up and, pre-empting the standard removal man's request, asked: 'Tea and cake chaps?'

The removal men set to with a will, carting boxes and creating their own pathway through the overgrown greenery to the front door.

Daisy went inside to find Frank and tell him about the two ladies she had met: The vision in tweed with Labrador and big nose and then the fast-baking cake lady. When she returned with cups of tea and slices of cake, it was gratefully received. The men all admitted that they had never been offered refreshment as promptly as that before and Daisy had to confess that it was a lucky coincidence for them.

Before returning to her unpacking in the house, she could not resist a short exploratory walk, as far as she could, into the garden. There was a sort of animal track worn through the undergrowth, that she followed until the brambles stopped her.

As she looked around, she was horrified by the carnage see saw: *Oh no! Someone has chopped the holly hedge down!* There it was... or wasn't! the remains of what had been a beautiful, six-foot-high holly hedge, was now reduced to about three feet. It had been brutally hacked down. It formed the boundary of their land and ran along the edge of the lane for about a hundred metres, providing a dense screen and now half of it was only a metre high, if that. Daisy felt so upset. It was certainly there last week when she had been up here with their surveyor to plan the alterations. *Why would somebody want to do that?* She thought.

    It took most of the day to unload the possessions needed in the short term, brought from storage. The children, knowing their parents well, had put the bed together downstairs for them in case it got too late to return to Christmas Cottage that night.
    Before moving in properly, they wanted to put two new bathrooms in upstairs and redecorate throughout, not to mention the new kitchen. It would be easy to work through the house with the rooms empty, so everything was stacked up in the old dining room and the whole room would be used as storage. What they didn't need now, could be moved by car, as and when they wanted it. For the time being it could stay at Christmas cottage.
    For some reason, it seemed to take a lot longer, with much more planning, to empty the contents of the removal lorry into the small cottage, than it had taken to empty the sprawling farmhouse. The removal men eventually left late in the afternoon, wishing everyone good luck in their new adventure. They were followed an hour later, by Sam, Ben and Louise, with their respective partners, tired and dusty from their efforts.
    'That's it, love. Just the two of us left for the evening.' They had a kettle, a bed, and lots of boxes. It reminded them of the early days and made them both laugh with nostalgia. 'Let's stay the night.' Frank whispered in a conspiratorial tone
    Early next morning, Daisy took the empty Tupperware box, washed clean, with a thank you note on top, to return to the kind lady who seemed a good soul. "Chestnuts" was halfway along the lane leading from the large village pond with about a dozen houses in between; some big, some small, most, with Manicured gardens. She set off walking and just caught a glimpse of who she thought was the cake lady, going into her house. Strangely, there was no answer to her knock on the door, so she decided to leave the Tupperware and note on the doorstep. *I hope it's the right house, it looks as unkempt as "Chestnuts".*

Daryl, the builder, arrived late the next afternoon, with a housewarming bottle of wine for his old friends, tucked in the large pocket of his cargo pants. Never ones to waste time, the Bests had warned him of the moving-in date, a week ago and he knew they would want to hit the ground running.

'Daisy!' Frank called. 'Darryl's here.' He was ushering the younger man in, past boxes and stacked building tools lined along the entrance hall. Daisy came hurrying through; they were both very fond of the young builder, who they thought of as a son. 'Hi Daryl. Thanks for coming so soon. Lovely to see you, is the family well? You busy as always?'

'Yes, lady Bee.' He always referred to her as that. Years earlier he had declared that she was 'always as busy as a bee!' And it had been a standing joke between them ever since.

'Pinot Grigio, Lady Bee.' He announced in a mock butler fashion, presenting the bottle to her, with a slight bow. She laughed as she accepted the offering. A kind thought.

While the lady of the house carried on trying to unpack and organise the kitchen, the two men headed upstairs and Frank ran through his ideas to refurbish the old building. A wall was to come down, a new one to be built, steel lintels to be fitted, new pipework for the new bathrooms, re-plaster all the walls.

'Start afresh is best, mate.' Daryl declared. He told Frank he could start the following Monday if it was convenient, before leaving with a long shopping list of materials that he would collect from the builder's merchants. Their friendship was such that he would always juggle his work about to fit them in quickly; they shared a mutual respect and trust. He would soon have the upstairs remodelled for them and it all gave Frank a focus. In the past, he had taken on all these tasks himself, but increasingly, he would have to let Daryl do much more, due to his constant eye problems.

Home improvements

Daisy decided to make a start outside. She phoned Brian, their trusty grounds man, who had worked at the farm over the years. He always did a good job and was young, strong and reliable, just what was needed. He came over and looked at the job, to give a price estimate. As a favour to her, he agreed to break his self-imposed rule and make a start at the weekend and then come back the following week; he would set about replacing all the fences and make new gates. 'Great! That's lovely, thanks, Brian.'

The smallest patch of garden was at the front of the house so that was the place to start. She set about chopping everything until she could see what was lurking beneath. It was like cutting though a jungle, constantly filling the wheelbarrow. She had already cleared a rough patch around the back and was stacking what she cut so that one evening they could burn it.

Now, this house had been derelict for a long time and the locals had grown used the sight of it. When they walked up and down the lane, they were naturally curious and so, it was, that everyone stopped to say hello and introduce themselves.

Daisy was in the front garden, filling the wheelbarrow for the umpteenth time. Frank had just repaired a puncture on it, it was the first practical thing he had done since his accident, almost a year earlier, and was feeling rather pleased with himself. There were so many thorns, it was likely to become a common event and he was taking a break to enjoy his wife's company.

'There you go, Daisy. Give that a whirl.' She pushed it round the back, tipped the rubbish out and returned to the emerging front garden.

'Okay now?'
'Good as new!' She answered with a laugh.

'Oh! Hello.' Said Frank, looking round, somewhat startled. With no peripheral vision, he was often taken by surprise by people standing to his side.

A woman, holding half a dozen dogs on leads, was standing in the lane by the broken picket fence, peering into the garden. She had been standing on his blind side.

'Hello. My name is Joan, I live in the village and I walk my dogs through here each day. Anyway, we are having a dinner party next Friday, nothing fancy, 7:30. Would you like to come?' Feeling hesitant, Frank answered: 'Oh, no I don't think we can, actually.'

'Oh well, we can change it to the following week. We are having it so you can meet us all.' She thrust a piece of paper in his hand and said rather forcefully: 'Ring me. This is my number.' She glanced at the garden. 'Do you like that privet hedge? Always reminds me of council housing, don't you agree? Anyway, you surely won't be keeping it?'

'Um, we don't know yet. We're just trying to get everything under control for now.'

'You'll like it here.' She continued. 'It's very pretty.'

He agreed: 'It is. And hopefully, when we have the garden under control, we will have a lovely view too. The houses are so attractive and most of them are beautifully kept, there must be some keen gardeners here.'

'You do know', she informed him, 'this half of the lane is private homes, the other half are tenants.' She waved her free arm dismissively in the general direction of the village pond. 'Those houses are owned by the Duke. He doesn't farm anymore but he still has all the cute little houses, so he rents them out. We laugh about them, the poor people. They think they are better than us because they live around the pond! But we know that we are better than them, because we are richer.' She laughed sarcastically. *How rude.* Frank thought. *Fancy coming straight out with it.*

Until now, he hadn't really looked at the visitor, but he saw that she was a tall, plain looking woman, one might say, almost asexual in appearance. Probably six foot; straight up, no curves, with a country- weathered face; dry and extraordinarily wrinkly. She wore a wax jacket with matching hat and exuded an air of self-importance… with the breath of a publican! Even from where she was standing in the road, it was hitting him. *Fancy walking up to a complete stranger and speaking that way.* He took an instant dislike to her: She was overbearing and bossy as well as being quite rude. *She wants to keep us in order!* He was a bit disappointed in the type of neighbour that they had met so far.

   That evening, Frank and Daisy discussed the dinner invitation. They both had a bad feeling about it but felt boxed into a corner by this forceful woman. Each day, as she walked up and down with her dogs, Joan peered in, looking for an answer to her invitation. Eventually, Daisy had no choice but to ring her. 'You know what Oscar Wild said: "if you're not at the table you're on the menu."' She said to Frank as she was dialling the number.
   'Yes.' he agreed. 'And if you ride on the back of a tiger, one day you get eaten! And Joan is definitely a tiger. Maybe I'm wrong but your gut feeling is usually right. Let's get it over and done with, we will go.' With the decision made, she pressed the button to set the dialled number ringing the pushy woman: 'That would be lovely, thank you. We would love to come to dinner on Friday.'
   'What do you drink?' said Joan.
   'Oh, we won't drink, as we will be driving. It's a bit far for my husband to walk at the moment.'
   'Oh!' She said, disappointment in her voice. 'That could be a problem. We drink and we drink a lot.' *I know.* Daisy thought. *Not only have we smelt your breath' but the drip with the big nose told me.*

Daisy's Best Friend

   Daisy's close friend Jenny, called by for a coffee and to look at the new house. 'Oh, I love it!' she enthused. 'What a beautiful spot. The garden will be amazing, I know you, Daisy. You and your green fingers. I can see it now: Bamboos swaying, sweet roses climbing the edge of the walks and green lawns sweeping down to the river's edge, you never know, the river must be somewhere near!' she added, optimistically. 'I can't wait for a nice summer's day, you know, when you dress the garden table: roses in bowls and white linen and the smell of the salmon cooking on the barbie with butter and herbs waiting to accompany the salad. And of course, the cold white wine.' She said with a suggestive chuckle. You will be happy here, how could you not be? it's stunning. I really am so happy for you, you deserve it, Daisy.'

The two had been friends since nursing together, years before. Daisy had been a very dedicated nurse and had been involved in many interesting and demanding, jobs. As Jenny reminded her of this, she admitted that it had been a privilege and she had met and worked with some amazing people. she recalled a memory as they sat with their drinks.

'Us two, drinking coffee reminds me of a story. I remember one day; I was working with the best bowel surgeon in the south of England. He was a very dedicated man…'

She had been with him all day in the operating theatre. it had been a hard day but fruitful and hopefully all the bowel cancers that day had been stopped in their tracks by the wonderful Bill. He had one more case, but he was exhausted. 'We sat and had a chat and I had made him a coffee. He told me that he had promised his wife he would be home in time to see the children before bed, and also, his wife had made him an "appointment with the lawn mower".' While the coffee cooled, they had gone through the notes of the final patient together. His, was an extensive cancer and it needed time and careful planning for a good outcome. 'We gathered his notes together, along with various blood results, X-rays and CT scan.' Off they went to the ward, Daisy giving moral support to the overloaded surgeon. Bill sat on the edge of the patient's bed.

'Mr. Barlow, shall I just call you Edward?'

'Please do.' The patient replied in a desperate whisper.

'Edward, I can help you. I am sure I can do the best job possible. It will take time and concentration. The truth is, I am too tired to attempt this now, at this late hour.' My plan is to go home and relax. I am going to have an early night so that in the morning I am refreshed and ready to tackle this cancer. I will see you at eight o'clock. How's that? Edward gratefully replied: 'That is so reassuring, thank you.'

'You sleep well. I will see you in the morning.'

They returned to Bill's office, piled high with notes and results. 'Right, Daisy. One last job, then we are done.'

Many years prior, in his clinic, Bill had met an elderly gentleman called Stanley, who had a bowel problem. During the Second World War, he had been a prisoner of the Japanese. He had been tortured and they had castrated him. His wife was now dead and obviously, they had no children. Stanley was elderly and alone. His story was horrendous and had greatly affected Bill, so although his bowel problem had now been resolved, Bill gave him an appointment once a month in his clinic, to check that he was doing well.

Daisy was Bill's theatre sister and the surgeon had told her on her first day, that if the lovely old chap, Stanley had a problem, big or small, she could arrange for him to been seen privately and Bill would settle the invoice. That was his promise to the war veteran, unconditionally, for the rest of his life. 'For what he gave to us in his service and for what he suffered as a prisoner of war,' Bill said the least he could do was to look after him until the end of his days. He had nobody. 'Sister,' he muttered under his breath in case any other patients might hear, 'can you make an appointment for him to see the eye surgeon please? his eyes have become troublesome. Get them to check him out, you know who to contact.' Then is his usual clear voice: Goodnight, my lovely Daisy, see you all in the morning.'

'What about Edward?' Jenny wanted to know.

'He came to theatre the next morning and Bill successfully removed his tumour and he went on to make a full recovery. And then, the next day, the same thing would come through the door again and Bill would tackle it the best he could. Amazing, kind, gifted man.'

'That is such a lovely story. Jenny was as big hearted as Daisy. 'Before I forget, I wanted to let you know that I can drive tomorrow, as you are so busy here.' They each took it in turn to drive to their volunteer job. Although they were both retired from the NHS, they remained firm supporters of the service and, along with other retired nurses, they all went once a month to the hospital as volunteers in the surgical wards. They made beds, made tea and made time for patients; all the things that had been hard to find time to do, when they were working. They loved it and so did the ward staff, who appreciated the extra experienced hands. They had been doing this for six years and it was their way of giving something back.

During her varied career, Daisy had also spent ten years, working for the police as one of the first Police Matrons. There she had been inspired to help some of the less fortunate members of society and was now a volunteer at the nearby prison. Some kids just made mistakes and a lot of these kids had never had any love, some of them couldn't read and write. Daisy listened; they loved her visits and she hoped their futures would be brighter. She helped them write letters every Friday and, of course, read the ones they had received. For the inmates, it was a welcome break from the boring prison routine. She always thought, when she was on her way home, how her own life was so fortunate, with the lovely Frank waiting at home for her.

Chapter five

The Dinner Party

Well. Tonight it is Joan's dinner party. Over the years, wherever they had lived, they had been very lucky and had always had good neighbours; the sort who look out for each other and keep an eye out if another neighbour was away. Frank had a feeling that Joan was somewhat disingenuous with her welcome. Nevertheless, they said they would go so that was that and as poor Frank could not see well at all today, Daisy would look after both of them.

The headlights picked out Joan's house through the murky darkness and Daisy parked the Land rover as far off the road as she could, mindful of Frank stumbling on the verge. During the short journey, it had struck Daisy that while the village was the shape of a spoon, Joan lived at the end of a long road, that twisted and turned like a snake. And here was her house, at the end: just like the head of the snake. *The snake's head, how apt! Lord help us!*

The front door was open before they had even got out of the car. 'Oh, good evening, do come in.' The Hostess was gushing. They followed her along the hallway and were shown into the sitting room, which was full of neighbours.

Joan's husband was away. He had been working on the oil rigs for years and, as she said; that was the way she liked it. Ironically, Joan didn't actually live in Whisperswood, but in the next hamlet, a cluster of 1930s council houses surrounding her own, somewhat older and slightly larger, pile.

Stepping into the sitting room, Daisy's eyes went round the room, as Joan introduced each guest to them. It was like looking round a room full of meerkats, all stood on hind legs, with their necks stretched, heads balanced on top, bobbing up and down, peering at the new faces. 'Frank.' she ventriloquised, 'We are the prey!'

The first, was the lady with the kind face, who seemed like a good soul (the cake lady) and her husband. They smiled politely but looked very much out of place, out of their depth, perhaps. Then there was the girl with the big nose, now sporting a bad fake tan (Who entertains the ladies of Whisperswood in her oak kitchen) with her husband, who coincidentally, had a big nose too. As they say, there is a lid for every saucepan.

Standing next to the 'Big Noses', were the MacDonalds, an odd-looking couple: her short and thin and him tall and fat. He looked as if he frequented the fast food company of the same name. She appeared as if life had got the better of her, or else her husband had! Her cup was definitely half empty while he was far too grand and self-important, to even say hello. *We'll have to earn a hello from him.*

'He is a parish councillor.' offered Joan, in a low voice, as if in explanation of Mr. MacDonald's imperious manner. In a confidential whisper, she added: 'We all call him "Moaning Mac.", he's such a miserable sod.' *Why bother inviting him then?*

Another couple seemed to be standing alone. They had nice, friendly faces. *The first ones!* The Bankses: Bunny & Eric. 'Cheers my dears. Lovely to meet you both.' Eric stepped forward to shake hands and said: 'We must get together sometime and have a jar.' as Bunny raised a large gin and tonic in greeting along with a smiling wink.

There was a single man, called Rupert, sitting alone in an armchair. His partner had died the previous year and the sadness of his loss still showed on his face. He seemed very pleasant; he was retired from banking but had the appearance of a man who spent his time in the sun rather than a stuffy office. He stood up to greet them, shaking hands just like a bank manager.

'Lovely to meet you both. I am afraid I don't do much these days, so you will see me pottering around the village. it's a lovely place to live. We are very privileged to awake to this each day, it's so pretty, each season.

'I sit and scribble out a few drawings, sometimes paint. Mostly local scenes. I went on a cruise a few years ago. You know what they say; "they are for the newly wed, over fed and the nearly dead". Well I didn't fit any of those, so I went to the art class each day. I really don't know how it seems to take some folks for ever to learn how to paint, I did it in a week! So that's how I spend my days. I saw a chap in the village sitting drawing in his garden and gave him a bit of advice. He was rather grateful and suggested I gave lessons and word got round so I do a few teaching sessions in my garden from time to time. When the flowers in are bloom it's glorious.'

'I like Rupert, Frank.' Daisy said under her breath as they were whisked away to meet the next guest.

'Me too.'

There was a very plump woman, who did not stop talking. She was with a much older, ruddy faced, man but Joan assured them that he was actually her husband, who spoke very little but made up for it by drinking as much as his wife talked.

Finally, there were the Joneses, an older couple. She was tall with protruding, horse-like teeth, rather gormless looking and almost devoid of conversation but did seem quite polite. Mister Jones had a bald head with a long grey curtain of wispy hair hanging from the sides. He was dressed from a 1976 C&A catalogue which they guessed, also explained the hairstyle. The Joneses seemed like an odd pair indeed. Neither Frank nor Daisy, caught their first names but hey soon realised that she barely uttered a sentence, leaving him to speak for them both. They were both full of themselves, but weren't they all? And there they were, all with their various degrees of snobbery.

The questions fired at the newcomers came thick and fast:
'Where did you live before?'
'What do you do for a living?'
'What car do you drive?'
'Any children? We don't really do children, in this village.' it was nonstop. In between the questioning, a few of the other guests gave the new neighbours their opinions and tips on life in the village. Mister Big Nose tried desperately to impress Frank with his knowledge of just about everything and failed dismally. As soon as he mentioned his interest in internet technology, Frank switched off and surreptitiously checked his watch, an old habit that he would have to break as he could no longer read the time from it.

'Dinner everyone!' Joan was calling everyone to order.

So, everyone filed through to a large, candlelit dining room and took their nominated seats the table. The prawn cocktail starter, which had been left standing all afternoon, arrived with great ceremony, in all its dried-out splendor. The assembled dinner guests worked their way through it, whilst most of them discussed how superior they were to each other.

But have you ever been somewhere when you think; *Why, oh why do these people hold their knives and forks in the wrong hand and cut in the wrong direction and then lick their knife? Oh my God. They are all sat at this table: the stuck up, snobby, posh, rich, not-so rich but all supercilious in their own way. And they can't use a knife and fork!* Daisy was feeling: *Get me out of here!*

The talk barely subsided as the main course of over-cooked chicken Kievs was served up, accompanied by undercooked greens and soggy boiled potatoes. Most of the diners were already quite well lubricated with alcohol and did not really notice the culinary failings.

'Anyway.' Joan said, as she sat back down: 'Have you met Mrs. Lupus?' directing the question at the guests of honour. The other guests all joined in: 'Oh, she is dreadful, a real problem in the village. She has had more letters from the Parish Council than you've had hot dinners.' Someone else added: 'We hope you will join us in writing to the local council, to complain about her hedgerow. It's grown into the road, scratching the cars and making the road narrow.'

It transpired that they had all made many complaints to the Parish Council Mafia via Mister MacDonald. Her house and garden, overgrown and in such a state of disrepair, was a source of embarrassment to the good citizens of Whisperswood. Frank and Daisy had indeed, noticed the out-of-control, hedgerow; it was hard to miss, not having been cut in many, many years.

Sadly, they had also realised that the lovely sunsets they had enjoyed at the farm, would not happen here, due to the neglect of Mrs. Lupus' hedgerow: it was now a row of trees so high that the sun only found its way through in faded, broken shafts, onto the row of pretty cottages opposite, "Chestnuts" included. A bit un-neighbourly, to say the least, in Frank's opinion. They were reduced to having the light on in the kitchen on the brightest of days and hoped that once they had sorted the little front garden and reduced the height of their own overgrowth, it may make a difference.

Oh God no! It was the old woman who had told us to "bugger off." She is Mrs. Lupus, the penny dropped. She was one of their nearest neighbours. *Great.* thought Daisy. She has been banging on my door this week, complaining about his lot at the table and they are complaining about her.

Everyone at the dinner party had plenty to say to the newcomers, Big Nose (male and female), more than anybody else. They learned that her name was Gail. *As in wet and windy. Certainly, full of wind!* It felt as if they were being shown their place in the pecking order. 'We have all lived here longer than you and this is the way things are.'

Two of the women were having a heated conversation about Japanese window blinds; one argued that you could see though them from the outside and the other disagreed. One had been on holiday to Botswana, the other to Cape Town and so it went on, trying to outdo each other. Frank leaned close to Daisy and whispered: 'This reminds me of "Abigail's Party".' The old play was a satire on the wannabe middle classes, they had seen it many years before.

Gail had had quite a bit to drink and was getting louder: 'I've sung six times with Des O'Connor!' She suddenly blurted out for no apparent reason other than no one was taking any notice of her.

'Oh! Were you a backing singer?' Asked Mary Mac, innocently, through a drunken haze. 'No, it was all on the same night, at one of his concerts. And I am a historian.' *Oh really!* And my parents have a country estate…' *God help us. Big nose, big mouth, big child!* She was so desperate to be important and liked.

'I can sing too.' said Mary Mac, enthusiastic for a moment. but Gail wasn't listening. She seemed very insecure, only interested in telling everyone in the room about herself. She was starring in the "ME show". Poor Mary Mac. seemed to shrink back in her chair and unhappily took another large swig of wine.

Bunny and Eric were slowly getting sloshed at the far end of the table. Everyone seemed to be ignoring them, so they were just getting on with it. 'Oh, I am so sorry, Joan. I seem to have knocked the vase of flowers over.' Bunny giggled.

'Ah don't worry.' Joan slurred. 'They're plastic. Just stand them back up.' It was like a game of skittles; the flowers went back up, then down. Exasperated at the situation, Eric suddenly growled: 'Bunny, give us the flowers!' As he grabbed the plastic vase and flowers in one large, boney hand and threw them under the table. 'Bunny,' he patiently explained, 'plastic flowers belong in the bin. Forget it, they're gone.' Looking up towards Joan: 'Hey Joan! Its a bit of a dry do down this end of the table. Give us a drop of something!'

The hostess pushed herself up out of her chair and staggered from her place at the head of the table, down to the far end, with half a bottle of whisky. She put the bottle heavily down on the table in front of Eric. 'Help yourself, handsome!' By some miracle she managed to stay upright and swivel through 180 degrees to make her way back to her chair. And so, the night went on.

The lady who talked a lot, appeared to have lost her husband, the old man who drank a lot. It turned out that he had just got up and left the table and nobody saw him again. He hadn't spoken to anyone anyway and she did not show any surprise at his disappearance. He rocked as if he was on a round base, like one if those kids' toys that when you push it down, just comes right back up.

'What are your plans for "Chestnuts"?' she asked Frank.

'Hopefully, we'll build a garage and then create some more living space.' he began.

'Oh, I don't know about that.' Interrupted Mr. Big Nose, with an air of authority. 'We had terrible trouble with the planners: "can't do this, can't do that". We really had to reduce the size we wanted to build. You won't get planning around here, too difficult.'

'Of course you can. He gets it all wrong, don't listen to him.' Joan interjected. 'I'm sure if you plan well, there will be no problems. Ask Moaning Mac., he's on the parish council.' *Ask him?* Frank thought. *He hasn't even said hello.*

The lady who talked a lot and whose husband had disappeared, drunk somewhere, continued: 'You didn't say, whether or not you had met Mrs. Lupus.' He had met her but kept that to himself. 'She is simply awful, don't take any nonsense from her, she is very rude.'

She told him that Mrs. Lupus hadn't spoken to her for the first ten years That she and her family, had lived in the village, simply because her children played pop music and in her, Mrs. Lupus', opinion, played it too loud. 'She made my life very uncomfortable, what a terrible thing to do a family. The only mistake we made, was moving here. She was so mean. It really did upset me, especially as nobody would come to my aid, they wouldn't cross the old bat. it was me against the world, I really did feel alone.

Joan was getting more and more drunk and was getting ruder, her po-faced, middle class facade had slipped and she was telling dirty jokes, badly. The posh accent had disappeared along with everyone else's.

Daisy was sensing that it was time to get out of there. She stood up and guided Frank round the table. 'We really must go. it's been a lovely evening and wonderful to meet you all.' She tried to sound sincere. They bid everyone a 'good night' and thanked Joan for the invite. As they were leaving, Bunny and Eric shouted above the drunken chatter: 'We must get together sometime.'

'Yes, we'll be sure to do that.'

The characters of Whisperswood were falling into place, sadly, none of them very impressive.

That night, lying in bed, the newcomers to the village lay chatting. What a night it had been: The one upmanship, the gossip and the very unkind things they had to say about those not present. It made them very uncomfortable and they vowed to be very wary of some of those who had sat around the table. There were clearly some people with too much time on their hands and a lot of big opinions.

Chapter six

Neighbours

With Bill, the plumber and Sam, the electrician, spread about the house working, it seemed a good excuse to get back out in the fresh air of the garden, tackling the endless chaos there. Chopping all day at the brambles and nettles was hard work but so rewarding. The pocket handkerchief patch they had originally cleared was now a respectable sized area. They had reached the two old half collapsed sheds that they had glimpsed on their first visit to "Chestnuts". Daisy hefted the sledgehammer and struck a well-aimed blow to the corner of the first shed and ran. Her aim was spot on and down it came with lots of noise, dust and even more laughter! The second shed collapsed in the same manner after only two or three more attempts.

The amateur but very enthusiastic, gardeners, were having such fun that the time had run away. When Bill called from the back door to say that the en-suite shower was up and running and that he would be back in the morning, they were surprised to realise that it was five o'clock already. Sam left in his van, a few minutes later, with a toot of the horn. He would be back tomorrow as well. The house was suddenly quiet, and it was just the two of them once again.

'Go and fetch a bottle of wine, Daisy. We'll burn this rubbish where it is.' Franks said, suddenly tired. He set to work, roughly piling brambles and other garden debris, on the remains of the first shed, to make a bonfire. She came back loaded with two glasses, a nicely chilled, bottle of white wine, some cheese and crackers and a box of matches.

The tinder-dry, rotten wood of the shed caught instantly, with the help of an old newspaper and in no time at all, there was a huge bonfire roaring fiercely. It was so hot that it consumed everything they fed it with no smoke, including the second shed and all the old gardening junk that had been in it for years.

They sat back on a pair of old garden chairs, brought from the farm, in the fading light. 'Cheers my darling.' The brightly burning fire illuminated their handiwork and lit the scene of happy contentment. They were dirty from the garden and now smelt of bonfire, as well. It was a wonderful way to enjoy their wine, knowing that they had a brand-new shower to try out before bed. This was blissful.

Invitation to Coffee and Brandy

Mrs. Lupus knocked, to inform Daisy that the woman from the red brick house up the lane, who had far too many children, had been outside Chestnut Cottage, chopping its hedge.

'She sometimes asks but generally just does just what she wants to. Give that one, an inch and she takes a mile! She's always looking for wood for her fire, she's fond of weed killer too. If she doesn't like it, she kills it. She chopped your holly hedge down, I saw her!' This was surprising news, they had not met the woman from the red-brick house, who had far too many children, but the old woman was so rude and blunt, that Daisy was inclined to believe her. She didn't seem the type to make up a story like that.   Daisy thanked her for the information and put her hand on the door to close it but the old woman made no move to leave. 'Also,' she continued, 'Joan keeps bothering me. Do you know Joan?' She demanded in her booming voice, peering through her bottle-end glasses, the lenses of which were so smeared it must have been like looking through frosted glass. 'Err, yes. I have met her actually.'

'She will keep calling at my house, with her bloody dogs, I don't understand why she is trying to befriend me. The word at the village shop, is that she had been stopped and arrested at the supermarket in town, for shop lifting. She had gone for her normal weekly shop and had slid a bottle of Gordon's gin in her bag and it wasn't the first time. It was in the local paper, all very embarrassing, but she has no shame. When she called by, she explained that it was all a misunderstanding. Of course it wasn't, she was nicking!' The way she emphasised the last word made Daisy suppress an involuntarily chuckle. 'There's nothing funny about it!' Mrs. Lupus stormed, glaring at Daisy.

The old crone continued her monologue. Now she was complaining that whilst they were chatting over coffee, Joan's dogs would dig holes in the garden. *how did she notice in that wilderness?* She did, however, concede that the gossiping visitor kept her informed of everything going on in the area.

Sometimes, the girl with the big nose accompanied Joan on these visits. Mrs. Lupus had a daughter who was a well-known singer in London's West End and Big Nose and her husband kept pestering the old woman to let them meet her. Mrs. Lupus was not keen. In some ways she must have felt vulnerable; she lived alone and was as old as Methuselah so, according to her tale, she had relented and arranged for her daughter to pay a flying visit to coincide with the Big noses being there at her house. It had not gone well; the daughter, realising that she had been duped into the meeting with a pair of fans. Daisy listened politely but really did not want to be dragged into these people's lives.

Finally, the self-opinionated old woman turned to leave and Daisy dared to breathe a small sigh of relief. 'Do come over for coffee tomorrow morning, we meet at ten. *Oh God no!* 'Come at ten and we will sit in the garden.' It was more a command than an invitation. *Just the once, I'll be polite. How can I really refuse?*

'Okay, I'll see if I can make it.'

Frank gave his wife a peck on the cheek. 'Wish me luck.' She said with mock horror as she stepped through the front door, bound for the Lupus rendezvous. It was a short walk from Chestnut Cottage to the entrance of the crumbling pile but it felt like an eternity to Daisy who really did not relish the prospect of Coffee with the old woman and her cronies.

It took a hefty push on the sticking, six-foot-high, rotting gate, before it gave enough to squeeze through into the hidden garden.

She entered the garden and there was Mrs. Lupus, flanked by Joan and Gail. Standing to one side was Mrs. MacDonald, who introduced herself as Mary and the lady who talked a lot. *I thought they didn't like each other but obviously, they do now.* Trying to remember who liked who was becoming difficult.

'Ah, good. Now we're all here, come and sit down.' Mrs. Lupus ordered. They all sat at an ancient garden table; Joan and Big Nose, pushing to ensure that they were one each side of the old woman. The table and chairs were under what must have been, at one time, a beautiful open gazebo, now slowly collapsing under the weight of neglected rambling roses and various climbing weeds.

It became obvious that Gail was like a sticking plaster: If Joan, a very forceful character, was there, Gail was stuck to her as if she gained confidence from her. She was her "yes man", agreeing with everything she said.

Mrs. Lupus disappeared into her disgusting, filthy looking, kitchen to make the coffee, while the five women sat making polite conversation about how lovely the garden was looking. *But it's just an overgrown mess!* It was only the odd patch of mowed grass that distinguished it from Chestnut Cottage's garden.

Mrs. Lupus' arrival with the refreshments, was heralded by the sound of her voice shouting at the various dogs to 'Make way! Get out from under my feet!' And then muttering loudly enough for all to hear: 'I don't know why people think they can just turn up with their dogs and spoil my garden.' Not only were her own three straggly haired mongrels there but Joan never went anywhere without her collection and Gail had brought her dog because she did not want to be left out.

The filthy wooden tray of mismatched, chipped mugs was dumped unceremoniously on the table and everyone was told to help themselves: 'They're all the same, sugar's in the bowl.' There was a little scramble to bag the cleanest looking cup and Daisy, not being experienced in the etiquette of Coffee at Chez Lupus, was left with a disgusting looking cracked mug with traces of food around the rim. The thought of drinking from it, turned her stomach. The bottle-end glasses worn by the old woman were perhaps not strong enough, or maybe she just didn't care, that that the cups were dirty; she was certainly none too clean herself.

    Daisy steeled herself to take a sip of the drink. The overpowering smell of brandy assailed her nostrils as she lifted the mug and as she took a sip the dreadful taste of cheap strong instant coffee with equal amount of brandy made her cough. 'Good God!' she said to Joan. 'Do you drink this?'

    'No, not always.' she whispered back. 'When she's not looking, throw it.' She took out a hip flask from her coat pocket and took a swig of something.

    'It'll kill the weeds.' Daisy said, with a chuckle.

    Mrs. Lupus, who was rather deaf, broke off her one-sided conversation with Gail: 'What's that, you two? Is your coffee strong enough Maisy?' *Maisy?* We always have a tot of brandy in it, it's the only thing that keeps Joan orf the bottle 'til lunchtime. Don't ever visit her in the afternoon, she's sozzled by then.' Joan's face clouded over with fury at this betrayal of what she thought, was her secret drink problem but she said nothing. The atmosphere froze for a couple of seconds until the old woman blithely continued: 'Do you like roses, Maisy? Everyone nodded in approval as Daisy answered in the affirmative.

    Now the conversation started to flow, as their attention turned to other neighbours in the village. One has just lost lots of weight; one is an alcoholic, she often disgraces herself at our drinks parties, this one 'is an utter bore!';

    'We don't invite those to parties, just drinks.' and 'We don't invite those to anything.'

    'Those ones are just holiday-home owners; the house is empty most of year. We don't like them, do we?' said Joan. There was a murmur of assent from the other women at this.

    'Anyway, that couple down the road from you, the Corbinnes, that's if they are married; really weird. She doesn't cook or clean. She certainly doesn't do fashion either.' she sniggered. 'Jane has no children, she's very precious. He does everything and that's not much! They call him Jerry, because he's like a mouse, after the mouse in Tom and Jerry.' She added in explanation. 'He always calls her Jane but that's not her name. Odd, very odd. Her mother is always there, cleaning. Of course, she's as old as the hills, talking away to herself whenever I see her.

'Perhaps if you said hello to her, she would talk to you instead of herself.' Daisy dared to interject. Joan ignored her and with a flash of annoyance, carried on with her rant as if nothing had been said.

'And then there is the lady gardener they have; a total fruit loop, plants all sorts of rubbish then never comes back to weed it. Of course, they can't afford to pay her, that's why. Jane stands watching her, always stuffing something in her mouth and when she's not eating, she is one of these annoying people who mine sweeps their mouth, first with her tongue, running it along the top front teeth and then back again and then with her finger, looking for the bits stuck in her teeth. The worst of it is, that she thinks she is so bloody posh.

'He's not so bad, compared to her, apart from being a creep but she always looks as if she needs a good wash. They both have ridiculous, matching peaked caps, Trotskyite things. They look like a pair of homeless, mature students, with those ridiculous open-toe sandals they wear all the time. They drive an energy saving car of course and she often has parking tickets on her windscreen, she never takes them off. She will be parked up in the village with them stuck on the windscreen. She leaves them on display because they've been issued at Oxford University or some such place, like some sort of trophy, I suppose. Oh my! she parks at the university. You get the picture. If the ticket was from Asda or somewhere, she would soon have it removed.'

You don't like them, then?

Daisy had been subjected to the forceful opinions of Mrs. Lupus and Joan with supporting comments from the other women, for nearly an hour and now she stood up to make her excuses and leave. Joan jumped up too. 'I'll walk Daisy to the gate, Mrs. Lupus.' They took a few steps away from the others before Joan asked, 'Are you coming tomorrow?' Daisy looked at her in surprise: 'What, you do this every day?'

'Yes.' she answered. 'Every day, from ten 'til eleven.'

'No, I couldn't. I am rather busy with my rental cottages, apart from everything else.'

Renting was profitable but kept Daisy busy even though she was renting just one, "Pudding Cottage", at the moment. Whether she was busy or not, she had more going on in her life than to waste an hour a day of it patronising a dreadful old crone like Mrs. Lupus.

'Oh! Oh well,' Joan was visibly disappointed, 'I'll walk you to the gate. I will have to go back and have a chat with Gail. Her husband sees himself as God's gift to women and he's been playing around with the babysitter. Naturally, Gail is a bit upset.

'For a young girl, she is incredibly nosy, so be a wary of her.' But so was Joan. She was left sat at home all day while her husband was away on the rigs and she appeared to be just as nosy. They seemed to Daisy like a good match.

'You see, Gail's husband is away all week, working in the city so I'm her only friend and I can tell you: she gets on my nerves, she can be so childish. Anyway, they got rid of the babysitter, she was the problem.'

The problem Gail has got, is Joan telling anyone who will listen, about the babysitter and Big Nose. They were the talk of the village. Mary Mac. had warned Bunny and Eric Banks, who had had no idea who she was talking about: 'Watch out, the babysitter is a man eater. You need to watch your man!' Bunny had laughed and told Mary that the girl would have to be pretty desperate to chase Eric!

While Joan was imparting this "private gossip", Daisy couldn't help thinking: *Why would the young baby-sitter be attracted to Mr. Big Nose?* He was a tall, skinny man with thin, limp hair, even limper, soft hands with long feminine fingernails. He was a loner, probably not by choice, an odd bod. She had Seen him walking by with his dog, definitely not the sort of man to catch a woman's eye, but there was no accounting for tastes.

'I'm sorry Joan, I really do need to be going.' as she edged further through the gate and back to normality. 'Okay then. But if you do change your mind about coffee tomorrow, we shall be here.' The gate crunched closed and she hurried back home to Frank.

'Never, ever again!' She told herself out loud, as she reached the sanctuary of her own garden gate.

Visitors

The garden at Chestnut Cottage was slowly rising like a phoenix, as the years of neglect were turned back, the wilderness tamed and new planting, under Daisy's careful supervision, created it anew. The house itself was coming together and was already unrecognisable from the near derelict property that had been for sale. The transformation was the talk of the village and it was difficult for the occupants to go out without questions from inquisitive villagers.

As promised, Ruby and Hugh, their old neighbours, had come over as the first visitors to see the new place. It had been a happy reunion with Daisy collecting them in time for lunch and taking them back home at midnight after a day of reminiscing.

Out of the blue, Lesley phoned from Harrogate: 'Chris and I have tickets for a show in the West End. Thought we would stop off on route, have a night with you and check the house out and perhaps you would think about coming with us for the weekend.'

'Just what we need about now, love.' Frank offered his opinion on the proposal. The two couples had been friends for some years but as they lived at opposite ends of the country, did not meet up as often as they would have liked. 'After all, we are supposed to be retired now.' They both laughed at this: Neither of them was the type to sit in a rocking chair, with their feet up.

It was true that they had been working flat out, recovering the cottage and especially the garden, as well as looking after their business interests. So, it was decided that they would have a weekend off and go with their friends to London. There followed a flurry of activity as they booked theatre tickets, train tickets and accommodation.

Lesley and Chris arrived at Chestnut Cottage, late afternoon the following Friday. After a revitalising cup of tea and quick tour of the house and garden, someone suggested that as it was such a pleasant evening, a walk around the village would be nice, before retiring to the pub for an early dinner.

The four of them set off walking at a leisurely pace, drinking in the scent of the countryside, whilst catching up on each other's news. The hosts were pointing out the various interesting pieces of architecture and nature to their guests, who were town dwellers and rarely saw anything so picturesque as Whisperswood.

Lesley was enthralled by the scene: 'It really is lovely here; the little cottages and gardens are so pretty. Who lives in that big house up the road from yours?' She enquired, looking back at the large, Georgian stately home that sat imperiously, on a slight rise, as if to look down on the rest of village. 'Oh, that is the Duke. He lives alone since his wife died many years ago. He has two sons who visit occasionally, they seem like pleasant guys. He's a very unassuming chap, utterly charming. Greets everyone he meets, he has no airs or graces.'

'But', Frank added, 'there is "Duke envy" here in Whisperswood. Because he is aristocracy, they all think they are as well! The closer they live to him, the closer connected they think they are. 'Gail, we'll fill you in on her later, told Daisy that his sons wave whenever they go by her kitchen window. "Oh my God they so gorgeous! Their clothes are amazing! and they make me weak at the knees!" Really! They all send him a Christmas card every year, with an invitation to their various drinks parties. He never goes but they all live in hope.

'It's very much a social climbing village here.' Daisy continued to explain. 'One night a week the "ladies" of Whisperswood meet to learn how to play bridge, which really means drinks and gossiping. I think anyone who isn't deemed rich enough, is ignored unless they need bums on seats for some event or other. And that's just from what they've told me themselves!

'According to Joan, I could write a book about this place.' She said absently.

'Sounds as if you should.' Lesley told her, enthusiastically.

'There are some very odd folk here and it kind of crushes the nice people.' She pointed out a small neat cottage: 'That is Suzy and James' house next to the Duke. They're a lovely couple, grandparents like us, so a busy life. I often see her, pushing their baby granddaughter in the pushchair through the village. That's Joan's house, right at the end of this long lane, you can just see the chimney tops. Not actually in the village at all. She still manages to be the village gossip though. And the village bully!'

Continuing their walk, they passed the Banks's cottage. 'That's Bunny and Eric's cottage, more of a house, really. Nice people, they still have some life in them.'

'Very grand looking.' Chris noted.

'It's lovely inside.' As Daisy said this, the living room window flew open.

'Hey where are you going? Eric shouted, leaning so far through the aperture that it seemed as if he would fall out into the garden.

'The pub for a bite to eat.' Frank called back.

'Well, grab a table for six, we'll be down in five minutes. See you there!'

'I told you they still have some life left in them!' Frank laughed. As far as he was concerned, it was the more the merrier. Six for supper, they got the last table, as there was a jazz band playing later that night, which always made for a full house.

Hardly had they sat down with their drinks, when Bunny swept in through the front door of the pub with Eric in her wake and made a beeline for the table. There were introductions all round and Eric declared that it must be 'my round by now, you four have been here ages!' They had a great night. The early dinner idea was forgotten as the conversation flowed along with the drink and the music.

As the band finished their final number, Eric, who was quite unsteady on his feet by now, invited everyone back to his place for a nightcap.

'We shouldn't really, but why not?' Frank and Chris answered, grinning, as one. The train tickets were open, there was no fixed reservation, so they could leave for London whenever they felt like it tomorrow. The late night turned into an early morning as the four friends staggered from Bunny and Eric's house, back to "Chestnuts".

The next day, feeling revived after a late brunch, they left for London. *Thank the Lord for nice neighbours and friends.* Leaving the car at Whisperswood, they took a taxi to the railway station, arriving just as the London train pulled in. With a lot of laughter and puffing, everyone raced over the platform in the nick of time, to be the last to jump aboard. It felt like being young again.

Their whirlwind weekend in the Capital, took in a great night at Ronnie Scott's club and a little-known musical production that was enjoying a limited run on The Strand. Naturally, they dined at Simpsons, which was conveniently opposite the theatre. While the men relaxed over slow coffees, their wives managed to squeeze a little shopping in.

Returning to "Chestnuts", it was agreed that Chris and Lesley should stay an extra night, as it was too late to hit the road back up to the north of England. It had been a good, long weekend, indulging themselves without a thought of the next job to do at the house and now, both Frank and Daisy felt ready to jump into the next task required for the restoration of the cottage

Chapter seven

Strange requests

Daisy was upstairs, tidying the front bedroom one morning, when, from the open window, she caught sight of Joan, hiding behind a tree, her collection of dogs straining against their leads as they tried to get back on the road. Daisy thought she must be waiting for someone and carried on with her chores. She didn't really have time to stop and talk. Besides, Joan only ever had gossip, usually vitriolic and she did not want to hear it.

After a minute or two, the semi-concealed woman caught sight of Daisy and waved. Then in a sort of shouted stage whisper, called out: 'Good morning.' Somewhat confused, Daisy returned the greeting. 'Are you waiting for someone?' She felt she had to say something. When the explanation came, it was even more surprising: 'I am just waiting for Mrs. Lupus to leave her house and take her mongrels out. I don't want to run into her, it's bad enough that we meet for coffee, without having to spend an extra hour with her, dog walking.'

'Oh.' What else could she say? *I thought they were best buddies.*

Joan was not leaving her hiding place but continued to shout up at the open window. It was no use; Daisy couldn't hear what she was saying, so relented and went downstairs, to open the front door. Joan peeped round from behind her tree, in the direction of Mrs. Lupus' house, before scuttling across the road, dragging the confused dogs behind her. She ducked into the front garden of "Chestnuts" and stood panting for a couple of seconds while she regained her veneer of middle class composure. "That's better, hopefully she didn't see me.'

'She wouldn't have. She left about half an hour ago. Whenever she walks her dogs, there is so much noise between the dogs barking and her shouting at them, that no one could miss it.'

'Oh. Nobody ever mentioned it to me before.' Joan mused, half to herself. For a woman who prided herself on knowing all there was to know about everyone, she suddenly felt that she had missed something.

'Anyway, have you made a complaint to the council about her yet?'

'No.' *We can hardly start to complain when we have only just arrived. That would make us as bad as the dinner party gang.* 'I'm not sure that we should turn up and start complaining. After all, we saw the state of her place when we viewed the cottage.' Daisy felt herself being pushed into a corner yet again, by Joan.

They were both distracted by the appearance of Mary Mac. *Thank goodness!* She was bustling up the lane towards them with a very purposeful air about her.

'Good morning.' She puffed. 'Lovely to meet you the other evening, Daisy. (it was a few weeks since Joan's dinner party) I am sorry I was so drunk.' She offered. 'I had taken a cold remedy and the wine went straight to my head.' *It sure did.*

Joan greeted Mary Mac. with indifference: 'This is a bit early in the morning for you, Mary. You're usually still hung over at this time of day.' Mrs. MacDonald either did not notice the sarcasm or chose to ignore it. 'Well, you know how it is,' She replied feebly.

Turning to Daisy, she breathlessly asked: 'Have you written to the council to complain about Mrs. Lupus yet?' Daisy had been too hasty in her relief at seeing Mrs. MacDonald. 'No. I was just explaining to Joan.'

'The other problem we have here, is the traffic.' Daisy looked both ways along the lane in disbelief. They hardly saw a car all day! 'Could I ask you to count the number of cars and take down their registrations, between eight and nine each morning and four and five in the afternoon?' *What?*

'We think it is the same people all the time, using our village as a rat run. Mister MacDonald wants them arrested by the police.'

'I don't think you can arrest people just for driving through a village.' *Dear God!* Daisy thought, *what sort of place is this?* In the few weeks since they had lived in Whisperswood, somebody had chopped their hedge down, they were required to complain about a neighbour and in their spare time, count cars. They were looking for fun and life. Passing their time with the neighbours was something they enjoyed but not like this.

Today, Frank had met the couple who lived in the red-brick cottage. As Mrs. Lupus had claimed, they did indeed, have a lot of children although not necessarily "too many", that was a typically spiteful remark. There were six sons, all well-built teenagers and the family seemed to burst out of the tiny house like some kind of party trick. No one knew what the living arrangements were, no one had ever seen inside, but they had to be quite cramped, if not to say, unorthodox.

It was while he was surveying the massacred holly hedge, that Frank heard a high- pitched, 'Yoo hoo!' behind him. He turned around, startled, to see the entire family of eight, standing in a row and leaning on their rickety garden fence, which looked as if it may collapse under them at any minute.

'Welcome to Whisperswood. We're the "Roses". Rose by name, rose by nature.' announced Mrs. Rose, in a giggling voice. She turned with a sweeping gesture, arm outstretched, as if to introduce her cottage, which was covered in roses of every hue, both climbing and rambling. Turning the other way, she 'introduced' the chaotic display of rose bushes that covered every inch of the front garden, all carefully weeded and pruned.

He didn't know if it was by design or accident, that they stood in descending height from left to right: which meant the diminutive Mr. Rose standing at the end next to his considerably larger, wife. He was about five feet tall, a rather quiet, thoughtful natured man, whilst his wife talked non-stop. She seemingly, had the ability to talk without pause or taking a breath, which she proceeded to do.

She was very proud of her achievement in chopping the holly hedge and readily admitted it when Frank casually mentioned that he wondered who the culprit had been. 'It was jolly hard work; I can tell you. It took me all day, out there on my own with saws, secateurs, all sorts of things. It used to stop the light coming into our house but now it's wonderful, you don't need a high hedge anyway, I don't have one!' The rest of the Rose family all nodded in smiling agreement. There was no animosity, they simply agreed with their mother's belief that it was her right to garden anything that she felt needed gardening, regardless of ownership.

'Actually, it is one of the things that attracted us to "Chestnuts." He told her, softly, although inside, he felt more than a little aggrieved.

'Well it'll grow back. Just wait and see.' She was very "matter of fact". To wait and see, was all they would be able to do, the damage had been done. Even with his poor eyesight, he couldn't see how cutting his hedge down to about three feet in height could possibly improve the light inside the red-brick cottage, whose windows were entirely covered by well-established rambling roses.

Mrs. Rose went on to say that they had inherited the cottage from an old Aunt, nearly thirty years ago. 'Of course, in those days we were just about the only actual owners here, everyone else was a tenant.' she elaborated.

According to her account, they had extended the cottage and installed electricity and running water. 'That's how bad it was. Of course, my Pod was much fitter then, weren't you Pod?' Mr. Rose nodded and gave his semi-toothed smile again. Homily, Mrs. Rose, said that he was fifty years old but Frank thought he could have easily passed for sixty-five plus.

'Oh yes. We had to cut and clear everything around in those days, no one here wanted to do it you see, so I made it my job. It was like your garden is now.' she said, standing on tip-toes, to get a better view into the garden of "Chestnuts", over the decimated holly hedge.

'I can always come around with one of the boys and clear those brambles for you, I have lots of good ideas for gardening. I'd have that cleared in a jiffy; we'd do that wouldn't we Wayne?' She rattled the words off like a machine gun, reaching up to ruffle Wayne's hair as she did so. The fifteen-year old Wayne looked down at his feet in embarrassment, the first time that any of them had stopped smiling.

'I could take away all the wood that I chop as well, for you. I'm always on the lookout for firewood, it's so much nicer than turning on the central heating don't you think? Not that we have central heating, or much of a bathroom really, do we Pod? Who needs it? The kids get a shower once a week at school when they have P.E. Pod never does anything, so he doesn't get dirty, Do you, Pod?' A shake of the head from Mr. Rose. 'I'm out in all weathers gardening so when it rains, I get a free wash. It's a perfect system, don't you think, eh?'

Frank now became aware that the wonderful scents of the massed roses were competing with the smell from eight unwashed bodies, along with the general whiff of decay, emanating from the cramped cottage.

Homily went into great detail, explaining what a problem Mrs. Lupus was, generally and especially regarding her neglected hedgerow, which was tumbling over and making the lane narrow, which in turn was creating a hazard for the traffic. She had crashed her ancient Morris Minor into another car, coming around the bend in the opposite direction, because the hedge was blocking her vision.

Later in the day, as Frank was recounting his meeting with the Rose family, to his wife, they both began to get the uneasy feeling that everyone here seemed to have a problem with someone. 'The Roses sound like "The Borrowers" to me.' That made him laugh. 'Yes, they are, I suppose. Let's just call them "The Borrowers", They have the same names after all.'

Chapter eight

Christmas

Before they knew it, December had arrived. There were no firm arrangements in place at Chestnut Cottage, for later in the month. The Bests had only been at their new home, a short while and were still enjoying the work of modernising the cottage and restoring the garden. They planned to spend the festive season with the rest of the family: Frank's father would be travelling down to join them from Newcastle, he was looking forward to staying in the newly decorated spare bedroom with the sounds of winter birdsong at the window.

Daisy's elderly parents lived nearby, so they would just come to Louise's house for Christmas Day, her partner would pick them up, where everyone was gathering to give gifts and enjoy a traditional lunch. By the time the adults had watched the Queen's Speech, the older generation would be ready for home, chauffeured by Daisy. Then it would be back home for a relaxing evening in front of the log burner.

Two weeks before the big day, it started: Invitations for Christmas drinks. It seemed that every time the letter box at "Chestnuts" rattled, there was another invite. In the ten days before Christmas, there were six drinks parties scheduled. How were they going to juggle this?

Daisy and Frank felt they were lucky. They had both worked hard, in successful, high pressure careers, before building up the farm and its bed and breakfast business. Once their children had flown the nest, they had found themselves caring for their own ageing parents.

All this had happened while they created a lovely home together. There had never been time to visit all their neighbours for drinks at Christmas, life had been too full.

Since Frank's accident, however, life had changed more than they could have imagined. His eyesight had become more and more of a problem and a large part of their life together, revolved around hospital appointments of one kind or another. They were quite able to manage but his lack of vision had knocked his confidence and he was a changed man in many respects. He felt overwhelmed by the pushy new neighbours, it was if they all lived as one: if one husband went to the pub, all the husbands went. Likewise, if one wife visited Mrs. Lupus, they all did. It was far too claustrophobic for comfort.

The world according to Joan

It was a crisp cold December morning and Chestnut Cottage would be seeing its first dinner party that evening. They had the morning free, so Frank and Daisy decided to make the most of the fine weather and get some fresh air, with a nice long walk. They hadn't gone very far down the lane when they met Joan, coming in the opposite direction with her usual pack of dogs. They exchanged 'Good mornings' and the usual pleasantries about the weather etc. and started to walk on but it was a bit disconcerting, to find that Joan simply wheeled her dogs around and fell into step with them.

'Now you <u>will</u> come to my drinks party this evening won't you.' As before, it was not a question but felt more like an order. This was the first they had heard of it and it was rather short notice. 'I am sorry,' Daisy excused them both: 'we will not be able to make it; we have our architect and his wife coming over to dinner.' She immediately regretted giving the gossip more information than necessary.

'Oh, bring them with you.' she insisted, 'It's all bums on seats.' *Why can't some people ever take 'no' for an answer?* 'No, really, we won't make it.' Frank told her with a note of finality. He found her pushy manner annoying.

As they walked up the lane, Joan now tagged along. 'I couldn't say the other day but Gail and her husband have a few problems, he works in the city all week, so once a week, they get a babysitter in so they can go out on a date night. Anyway, she caught him and the babysitter kissing in the car.

'It was after they got home from Nando's.' She emphasised "Nando's", with heavy irony. 'Yes, I know!' She added, rolling her eyes. 'Some people do think that's a nice place to go for a meal! Anyway, *One of Joan's favourite words,* he was supposed to be running the babysitter home and Gail noticed that the girl had left her gloves on the sofa. She ran out to the car and there they were; kissing in his car. Snogging, in fact.' She added to stress the gravity of the scene.

Poor old Big Nose. Daisy thought. 'Problem is,' Joan continued, 'she is home all week on her own, she's bored and for a young girl, as I told you before, she is incredibly nosy. She has a daughter but she is at boarding school, so Gail just wanders round looking for company. He bought her the dog, you must have seen her up and down with the chocolate Labrador, it's called "Truffle".

'When he's home, he tries hard to fit in as a country gentleman but he doesn't; he's too much of a big head, drinks too much, then he gets loud and mouths off, he's an idiot.' She was getting more disdainful about him as she spoke. 'Anyway, the thing is: her family is pretty well off, he's married into it and it's all gone to his head, he just cannot stop bragging. I have the feeling that her Daddy's money might run out and if it does, he will be running out soon after! So anyway, she comes to Mrs. Lupus' every morning with me.'

'But I thought you didn't like Mrs. Lupus, you asked me to write to the council and complain about her.' Daisy was still rather confused about the dynamics of the relationship between Joan and Mrs. Lupus, although things were becoming more obvious to her.

'That is two separate things.' came the reply, sharp, as if to a naughty child. 'The point is; her daughter has asked me to look out for her and asked me to have a power of attorney for her mother. Should anything happen, for instance, if she was ill, she is worried that there would be nobody around to sign things if she needed treatment. The daughter lives in London, I don't suppose you know that. She won't let me control her money though.' This with a hint of bitterness. 'Anyway, her daughter is paying me a wage to care for her. Well you don't think I would do it for nothing do you?' She exclaimed, seeing the look of shock on Daisy's face.

So, Joan could not stand Mrs. Lupus, who did not have much time for her either but her daughter thought they liked each other! So, she was paying Joan to spend an hour a day with the cantankerous old woman.

Joan had already told her that she sat in Mrs. Lupus' garden under a wooden canopy come rain or shine, drinking coffee with brandy in a dirty mug. She had never mentioned that neither of them liked each other!

'I have never been in the house though. I think she is too ashamed of the state of it.' I once peeped in though the back door when she wasn't looking and there were plenty of mouse droppings about. Probably rats as well, come to think about it. Mind you, she has some valuable paintings in there. I've seen them through the window.' Daisy had glimpsed the kitchen through its dirt crusted, window and had to agree.

'Anyway, who else was at the dinner party? Oh yes, the Joneses: Mrs. Jones with her dreadful teeth. With all their money, why doesn't she get them fixed? She's okay; snooty and long suffering. She doesn't say much because there isn't much going on inside her head. Her husband has little-man syndrome, he constantly belittles her in front of us. Actually, I think he fancies me.

'Now he, Mister Jones, throws lots of drinks parties. He's rich, retired and a prolific letter writer, he complains about holes in the road, houses being built in town, river pollution, poor people living too close to him… anything. You name it, he writes about it to each authority.

'Invites to his house are quite regular because he's bored. The problem is, he has wandering hands so be careful. I couldn't tell you how many times he's tried it on with me, the randy old bastard.' She fluttered her thin, pale eyelashes as she said this. *Her face is like a Relief map of the Alps it's so wrinkly. Surely even Jones couldn't fancy her!* The thought of Mr. Jones in all his old aged nineteen-seventies' glory, making out with the frigidly, asexual, Joan repulsed her captive audience of two.

'The MacDonalds: she is the village gossip. If it's happened in the village, Mary Mac., we all call her that, will know all about it and tell everyone. They don't have two ha'pennies to rub together, that's why she always has a few vegetables or apples for sale outside. Not outside her own house, mind you, that would never do! No, she sets her little stall up outside the cottage next door, with a money jar to take the payment. The slightest movement in the lane and she will be out, in case there is any gossip to be had. I don't know who she thinks she is fooling, that cottage has been empty for years. Yes, she's a sad case, alright.

'Moaning Mac. is the parish councillor in charge of the village sports field. He invented that post himself. He is the last person one would expect to be involved in sport; he is such a sloth. If you ever see him do anything faster than dead slow, you should ring the papers.'

'Do you mean that field on the left, as you come into the village?' Frank asked her. He had not really been paying attention to the constant monotone gossip.

'Yes, of course!'

'But it's just a sloping meadow.'

'Don't let Moaning Mac. hear you say that!' She gasped. 'He has big plans for that "meadow". He fancies himself as a cricket umpire and that is his personal little empire. The old cow shed at the top of the field is his cricket pavilion and he's trying to get sponsorship to fix it up and get the grass mowed properly.' *Ridiculous!* Frank said nothing and kept his opinion to himself.

'The parish council is the only other thing he's interested in. They have a son, you know. He turned out to be gay, so old "Moany" kicked him out. He's living up North now, with someone he met up there and they have a child, I don't know how. Mary is always wanting to go up there, to visit her sort of grandson but the old bore won't hear of it.

'Anyway, don't tell anyone but he can be a real pain in the backside for everyone, not just his family. He has upset a lot of people round here in the past. Eric Banks, who was at my dinner party, had a letter from him: It was a notelet, the type that you can get printed on the internet. On the front there was a picture of him leaning against the wall, posing like some mean and moody, old age model. Ha-ha!' She could not help laughing at the thought of it. Inside it said:

Eric.
We all get along here, but you keep parking your car near my house and it
annoys me. It makes it difficult when our online delivery arrives.
Yesterday, the online delivery truck could not park to deliver Mary's order.
Your Neighbour,
Mr. MacDonald (Parish Councillor, Cricket Umpire.)

Daisy and Frank actually, already knew all about the letter as Bunny had shown it to them. At the time, Eric had felt terrible as their house was a holiday home and being desperate not to upset anyone, he had apologised profusely to the self-important Parish Councillor.

By coincidence, the Bankses had a delivery themselves, the very next day. Bunny rushed out to catch the driver: 'Hey,' she said; 'I'm really sorry if we blocked you the other day.'

'Ah, it was fine, you didn't, at all.' he explained. 'There was plenty of room, just Mr. MacDonald having a go for the sake of it. Every time I have a delivery for them, he's got a problem with something! What else would he do with his day? Anyhow, I bet he wouldn't want anyone to know what I'm delivering. Think about it, madam, we get to know what's in a delivery!' raising his eyebrows suggestively. He quietly laughed to himself as he got back in his van while Bunny stood there holding her parcel imagining all the things that the boring Moaning mac. Get up to in private.

Bunny had felt relieved but annoyed at Moaning Mac., who was always having a dig at her and Eric.

Joan continued her lecture: 'He's okay as long as you don't cross him, and most people seem to cross him, somehow.'

'You don't think, maybe, that he crosses them?'

The older woman paid no attention to the question, she was still in full flow: 'I don't actually like those Banks people, they're far too rough to be living in Whisperswood. Between you and me, I only invited them to find out what they are like, they only moved in a few months before you arrived and none of us knew anything about them. Do you think they have any money?'

'Where did the man who drinks too much go? We never saw him again, that night.' Daisy tried to steer the subject in a slightly different direction.

'Oh, he's just rude. We don't really like him, he just comes along with his wife, he's about twenty years older than her. He always disappears once he's had a few gins. She says he's always there in the morning, so she doesn't worry about it.' *Each to his own.*

'She's a secret drinker anyway, although she tries to hide it from him. She works so hard trying to scrape a living from A.I.R. B.N.B.' Joan spelled the letters out individually.

'You mean Airbnb?' Daisy asked, laughing. This provoked an angry frown from Joan but she made no comment.

The gossip continued as if no one had said anything: 'She packs him off to the West Country somewhere, to see his other old man friends, then we get on the bottle together.' Her face clouded again for a second. 'I shouldn't have said that. I <u>didn't</u> say it!' But she <u>had</u> said it and of course, it was the truth.

The cold was creeping through Daisy's overcoat and under her scarf now, as Joan had slowed their brisk walk to a dawdle. The more intent she became on her gossip, the slower she walked.

'Well, I'm afraid we must be getting back, we've a lot to do…'

'I've been married twice, you know.' Joan was not letting them go that easily. 'Both useless but at least this one is never home; he just pays the bills. I talk to him by Skype but I don't turn the camera on, that way neither of us has to look at the other.

'I'm so bored, you know, I walk these bloody dogs for miles. There is a limit to how many dinner parties I can throw, even though everyone thinks I'm marvellous at it. *Self-praise is no praise.* As if realising that she was letting her confident facade slip, she changed the subject to the cake lady, who seemed a good soul. 'Oh, she's alright for cleaning the church or running errands but…'

'I'm really sorry, Joan, Frank has to have his eye drops put in. We <u>must</u> go.' Daisy interrupted. Even she knew, as she said the words, that it didn't sound like a very genuine excuse. They bid each other a good day and parted company, Joan calling behind them: 'Do try and bring your friends along tonight!'

The constant gossip was beginning to get so wearing. They understood that they were new and an object of interest but boy oh boy, it was as if everybody needed to get in first and let them know about this and that. It was all so negative and one thing was certain: They would not be subjecting their friends to drinks at Joan's.

Chapter nine

Friends

Back in the sanctuary of "Chestnuts", Daisy put the kettle on and Frank lit the log burner. It was one of the first things they had fitted, shortly after they moved in. The comfort of its glow transformed the living room into a cosy haven that tempted a person to just sit and relax on a cold day. Of course, it saved money as well; they had plenty of wood stacked in the garden as they cleared the grounds, so it was a win, win, situation.

'Fancy saying that about the eye drops!' He laughed.

'I was too cold to think of any other excuse.' Daisy said, joining in the laughter. That woman's the limit.'

Within no time, the cottage felt so snug, as the heat from the log burner, spread through the rooms. Working as a team, they started to tidy the house and prepare the food for the evening's dinner. Their long-standing friends, Bob and his wife, Alison, were coming for supper. Daisy loved cooking and preparing the house to entertain and certainly, the cottage was beginnings to look homely. They had achieved a lot in a few months and all their friends were keen to see the fruits of their labours

Bob had been the architect on several building projects that they had undertaken in the past and tonight they would almost certainly end up discussing ways to improve Chestnut Cottage. The two friends had always both been on the same wavelength and enjoyed bouncing ideas off each other. Frank knew that Bob would not contemplate a visit, without bringing a sketch book and pencil – just in case!

The food was ready and as the wine glasses and flowers were placed on the table, the doorbell rang; the guests had arrived. It was great to see their old friends as they welcomed them into the new home.

Daisy thanked Alison for the beautiful bouquet of flowers that they had brought, and they stood chatting in the kitchen while she finished making the gravy for dinner. She confided in her that Frank had fallen down the stairs twice and that his eyes were getting no better as they had hoped.

'It's a new layout, I'm sure it will get better as he gets used to it.' Alison said, trying to reassure her friend. Perhaps she was right.

She poured her heart out to Alison about settling into the village; how she missed her old neighbours and how it just didn't feel right here. The neighbours were so judgemental, overpowering and so demanding: constantly wanting them to share their opinions and have none of their own. If they did voice any opinion, they were knocked back. She related the tale about the night they had met Joan's gang at the dinner party and how uncomfortable it had made them feel.

'It will be okay, it's just new. You see, at the moment you're New, they are curious. They will tire and find something else to focus on, most of them are too rich to work, and if not, too old so they have nothing to do all day long.'

'It's like we can never refuse an invite. It's Christmas, I have a million things to do.' she explained.

'Look,' said her friend, 'forget about them and stop stirring that gravy! Let's join the chaps and have a glass of wine.

Christmas drinks

Today was the Jones's Christmas drinks party. At a quarter to two, Frank and Daisy set off for the two o'clock start. Daisy said: 'Oh come on, Frank, we might enjoy it.' as they left "Chestnuts".

After a couple of minutes' walking, they fell in a few yards behind the Roses from the red brick house, with their, according to Mrs. Lupus, "far too many children". They were also walking to the Jones's drinks party. As they walked down the road, it seemed as if this quiet country lane now had a walking bus, with folks joining it, until they reached the Jones's fairy-lit house, where there was already a row of people waiting to be let in from the cold.

'Now these, are serious party people.' They whispered to each other as they were ushered into the large house. Immediately upon entering, they were faced with a temporary clothes rail, lined with hangers, to take everyone's coats. A computer-printed sign asked them to "please leave your coat here". Adding their coats and hats to the row already hanging there, they saw the next sign, standing on a small, purpose made post: "please remove your shoes". There, next to a shoe rack, was the biggest pile of new hotel slippers from every hotel one could think of.

Dressed to party, "the Jones way", they walked into the reception room and couldn't help a chuckle at the scene. The guests were all walking around the Jones' house in matching white hotel slippers. It was a practical idea to protect the carpets but it really did look rather ridiculous.

Off the reception room, was another large room totally fitted out as a bar, complete with hired in staff to serve the thirsty guests. The neighbours all got stuck in to the drink. And boy did they drink! There were nibbles, mainly sausage rolls and mince pies being offered around by more, young hired-in staff.

They had hoped that Bunny and Eric might be there, for some interesting conversation but they were nowhere to be seen. Mr. Jones came up, looking as ridiculous as ever, his bald pate polished to a parade ground gloss, in contrast to the grey curtain of hair carefully combed down to brush his shoulders. He was once again dressed head to toe, in faded designer clothes from the 1970s: plenty of money but no style and they supposed that in his heart, he was still twenty. If only he would just cut the hair at least!

'Now,' he said to them, 'you must let me show you round. This is our sitting room. Rather large, I know. Just look at the view, it's wonderful to wake up to, I never tire of it. Most people would give their right arm for that view.' And so, the house tour continued, even including the master bedroom, decorated in deep red flock wallpaper and boasting a mirrored ceiling. The tour ended with: 'This door leads to my garage. I have quite a collection and I only buy cars that are silver in colour. Like my hair!' he said with a lecherous tone, looking at Daisy. Fortunately, the key to the door that would have opened onto his automotive pride, was not in its lock and they were spared any further one-upmanship. Jones had made his point: I may not be much to look at but I think you'll find I am the wealthiest man in Wisperswood.

'Do mingle and find yourself a drink.' he said, attempting to stroke his left hand down Daisy's back, as he turned to greet a newly arrived couple. The "grand tour" had taken the best part of half an hour and the party room was now fairly packed with guest; all in white hotel slippers. The hum of chatter over Mr. Jones's CD: "The Best Of The Seventies Christmas Hits", made it hard to hold a conversation.

Mrs. Rose stopped by for a chat, a glass of mulled wine in each hand and her mouth full of mince pie. 'You have been busy in the garden, I see. It's all looking a bit clearer; I can see right in now. you will have noticed we have chopped the holly hedge back, never did like that hedge. Now we can wave when we see you.'

'Yes, Frank told me it was you. Well we do like it, actually and we understand that the place has been neglected for years but we will keep it all under control, so please don't cut it again. It takes years for holly to establish itself into a fine hedge and a good shape.'

'Okay.' said Mrs. Rose, totally unfazed. 'More wine? I am just going to get us another, you have to dig in while its free, don't you?'

'Oh, not for us, we are popping over to see the grandchildren later.' Looking around the room, they could see the entire Rose family scattered around, each one holding a drink in either hand. At least the two youngest, thirteen-year-old twins, only had Cokes!

Now the lady who talked a lot and her husband who drank a lot, were standing in front of them. 'Oh hello!' she gushed. 'Are you leaving already?' Her husband grunted an acknowledgement, spitting sausage roll as he tried to speak and eat at the same time but was already too drunk to communicate coherently. *He'll probably disappear soon.*

'Yes, we are going to see our grandchildren, it's been arranged for months.' Daisy explained.

'Oh!' she sighed theatrically. 'I have a friend with grandchildren, it's all she talks about. I call people who do that "granny bores". She went on to say that she had two daughters and how amazing they both were, one was a 'simply super horse woman', who had her eyes on the British Olympic team. The other, had never actually done anything since leaving university three years earlier but she was also, wonderful! *Umm. Wait until you're a Grandma, because at the moment, you're a mother bore!*

'Changing the subject, are Bunny and Eric Banks here? they seemed a pleasant couple.' Frank remarked. 'No, they are only here on high days and holidays.' she told them. 'They're rough, don't you think?' It was Joan shouting over, breaking off her conversation with someone else, to interrupt. Daisy pulled Frank gently by his cuff. 'Time to go.' She whispered discretely. They weaved through the, mostly tipsy, guests, to find the host, Mr. Wandering-Hands Jones and his wife. The Joneses drunkenly tried to persuade them to stay but they made their excuses and left.

Walking back to "Chestnuts", it was just getting dark and they were picking their way along the lane avoiding the frequent piles left by horses from the nearby stables.

'I really do not like all this gossip, Frank.'

'Gossip isn't always hurtful but it is always bad manners.' Frank remarked quietly, his thoughts elsewhere.

'Oh God Is there anybody normal here?' Daisy wondered aloud. At this, her husband gave her a reassuring hug with one hand around her shoulders as they walked.

There it was: Another drunken affair, same crowd, same drunks.

New Friends

The Bests had bonded well with the Bankses on the several occasions they had met up together. Both couples enjoyed the other's company and the conversation always flowed easily; nothing heavy, just lighthearted chat, a bite to eat, a couple of drinks and a laugh.

'Come on, we'll walk down and put a Christmas card though their door, they'll be back in a couple of days for Christmas.' Daisy was standing, tiptoe on the front doorstep, sprinkling salt on the path beyond. She was always afraid that Frank would slip as he couldn't see the ice. Of course, the postman also used that path and it would never do for him to take a tumble.

'Morning!' Called a couple who had stopped at the cottage gate. 'I am sorry.' the lady said. 'We don't know your names.' as she reached over the gate to hand a Christmas card to Daisy, who ventured down the frozen path towards her.

'We are Alice and Matthew; we live at the top of the lane. We just wanted to welcome you both to the village and wish you well and hope you have a lovely Christmas.'

'That's very kind, thank you. I have seen you walk by; I think we have bumped into most people in the village. You must live near Joan.'

'Oh, no. Joan and her husband, we don't know his name; he works away, they live in the next village but unfortunately, everyone knows her. She spends her day walking her dogs and gossiping, that's who she is. I believe she has just joined the parish council so she will be ruling the roost over us all soon. We don't get involved with her, that's the safest way to deal with people like that.' *Good advice.*

'Have you met Bunny and Eric Banks? They're not always here though.'

'Yes.' Daisy replied. 'They're a lovely couple. We are actually just on our way to post them a Christmas card.'

'Well, have a super Christmas. Nice to meet you.' They both gave a friendly wave as they resumed their walk. 'You too.' Daisy called. *Now they seem more like the kind of neighbours we like!*

She went back in, to help Frank with his coat and scarf. Wrapped up against the cold, they carefully trod the newly salted path out of the cottage and set off walking, delivering a few cards as they went.

That evening, they were to go to the MacDonald's for Christmas drinks. 'Come on Frank. Last one.' They knew the routine by now: Mulled wine, sausage rolls, mince pies and more gossip.

'Come on.' she repeated. 'As my mother would say: "If you're going to do something, do it with a good heart."' She had made a nice golden tassel to decorate a bottle of wine enough to make it Christmassy, as a gift for this evening's hosts.

Bearing the gift and once more, muffled against the weather, they left the comfort of Chestnut Cottage by the front door, resplendent with its freshly made Christmas wreath, out through the little picket garden gate and hey ho, the walking bus was coming: Joan, Mr. and Mrs. Big Nose, the Roses, The Joneses and there would surely be more as they walked. Everyone kept a polite distance from the group in front as if no one wanted to use up their conversation before arriving at the drinks venue. It was a ten-minute brisk walk to the MacDonald's cottage and indeed, everyone in the walking bus did walk briskly, to keep warm. Even for the time of year, it had seemed exceptionally cold and dark, all day.

On arrival at Chez MacDonald, guests were directed to the spare bedroom at the top of a narrow, creaking staircase, where they could leave their coats on the bed. No formal rail and hangars here. Relieved of their outer clothing, they each retraced their steps until they reached the kitchen, at the base of the stairs, where Mary Mac. was stirring mulled wine in a large aluminium, saucepan. She had run out of wine glasses, so was serving the warm wine in sherry glasses, a faux pas, which was not lost on Joan.

Frank and Daisy followed the sound of conversation until they found the other guests, squeezed into the dining room and made the same small talk as at the previous get togethers. All the usual faces were there but tonight with the addition of Jane and Jerry Corbinne, who had avoided the previous sessions. They lived a few houses along the road from Chestnut Cottage and although they had never met, Frank had an idea of what to expect, after a chance meeting with Jane's sister. It had happened after the postman had a left a parcel, addressed to Jane, at "Chestnuts".

Her sister had come round to collect the parcel because the postman had left one of his little cards that say: "Your parcel has been left at Number 2, or whatever". She had explained: 'I am sorry to bother you like this. Jane never thinks about anybody but herself, it's just typical of her to order something off the internet then go away when it's going to be delivered. They're on holiday in Benidorm for two weeks but she'll probably tell you they went to somewhere upmarket so they could read books or something.'

Jane's sister was such a nice lady and evidently, glad of someone to chat to and share the annoyance she felt at her sibling's shortcomings as she carried on: 'She thinks she's so la-di-da since they moved here but neither of them have an ounce of common sense and they're both so lazy! But don't say I told you so.' She said seriously. 'I've just been in there and the heating has been left on full blast, it's like the Bahamas. Do you know? the back door wasn't even locked!

'I have been doing the washing up, I had to: the dirty dishes were stacked up in the sink and with the heat, everything was covered in mould and it was stinking. I only came to check on the house, but I'll be there all day!' She thanked Frank again for taking in the parcel and listening to her tale of woe. When she had gone, he could not help feeling disappointed at the type of people he had drawn, in the lottery of neighbours. They did not seem like his kind of people.

Jane was a buxom woman, with a disproportionately fat backside. She thought herself very superior in general, because she had taken a degree in her forties and was now some kind of academic. She was careful never to let on, what exactly she had done before hand. Joan claimed that she had been a Tesco checkout assistant but although a couple of the gossips had corroborated this, no one was really certain, until Jerry let slip that it was true but that she was now a filing clerk at the council offices. Frank and Daisy really did not care.

They had not been at the MacDonald's Christmas drinks for long, before Frank nicknamed Jane, "Yah Yah". Her affected nature was such, that she seemed incapable of simply saying 'yes' but answered everyone with the over-the-top exclamation. When she patronised him at being "so sweet", for decorating the bottle of wine, the quality of which, was far superior to anything on offer from the

MacDonalds, that they had brought, she went too far. 'My thing is Guacamole.' She gushed. 'I brought a bowl of it tonight for Mary.'

'Actually, it's the only thing she knows how to make, I'm afraid.' Jerry bravely ventured. She shot him a withering glance that silenced him instantly and his eyes fell to the ground. 'He does the cooking, I'm far too busy for anything like that. We are vegan, so it is sometimes difficult eating out, it's easier for him to prepare something for me.' She had managed to eat plenty of Mrs. MacDonald's beige food, however and was now "minesweeping" around her mouth with her tongue, cleaning up remnants still stuck to her teeth... Just as Joan had described.

Jerry went to speak again but she just talked over him. Fortunately, the awkward moment was saved as Mary Mac walked over and offered them the choice of a glass of *Blue Nun* or beer from her hostess trolley. Jerry put a hand out towards a can of beer as Jane said: 'No! He drinks red wine only, now we are together, don't WE.' Staring hard at Jerry. 'Yes, yes, that's right.' He stammered. *Poor man. Bet he would have loved a beer or even a white wine, but Jane has spoken!*

Joan swanned over. 'Well, what do you think, pokey little cottage, eh? Anyway, she makes great sausage rolls. Every cloud has a silver lining!' *God this woman was impossible.*

'Have you seen Jane and Jerry? The state of them! they must have thought it was a fancy-dress party!

'No.' lied Daisy. She didn't want to indulge Joan while she gossiped about yet more neighbours. Hopefully, she would move on and collar someone else.

Moaning Mac walked past them, surveying his guests with a self-satisfied smile. He may have been the host but he still did not speak, or even acknowledge them. He was retired, they didn't know what from, but he played cricket, "badly", his wife said, although no one had ever seen him participating in the game. It was perplexing that they had been invited here for drinks and nibbles only for the host to ignore them.

The cake lady, who seemed a good soul, was there with her husband, Justin. They said they were looking forward to Christmas, but they didn't have much to chat about, they were suffering from

Christmas drinks fatigue. Having attended every drinks invitation, they were sick of the sight of sausage rolls, no matter who had made them and had run out of conversation. They announced that they had things to do and would have to leave early, after less than an hour of the MacDonalds' dubious hospitality.

The evening was pretty flat and the Bests were thinking of an excuse for themselves to leave, when the Big Noses rocked up with their fourteen year-old daughter and things hit a new low. 'Hi! How are you two?' Mr. Big Nose commenced. 'Oh, fine.' Frank replied, looking into the half full wine glass he was swirling in his hand. 'How are you?'

'Fine, fine.' Enthused Mr. Big Nose. Gail, chimed in with: 'This is Tiffany.' Standing with her hands protectively on Tiffany's shoulders. 'Tell Frank and Daisy what you are getting for Christmas, darling.' The precocious child held up her left hand and ticked off fingers with her right, as she recited the list: 'A quad bike, a new laptop, the next iPhone...' But most of all, she was going to have a much desired, nose job. she was only young but was very aware of the unfortunate inheritance from her parents. 'Daddy helped me design it on the computer, as it is his job: technology.'

'Wow!' Daisy patronised her, 'That's nice.' She thought to herself, *Did I just say "nice"?* She was shocked, to say the least. A fourteen-year-old, having rhinoplasty! It was unlikely that such a procedure would be carried out on someone so young, maybe they were planning to have it done abroad. Daisy had looked after herself over the years and had had a few small jobs done here and there but she was grown woman, not a child.

As soon as the cake lady, who seemed a good soul and her husband left, Daisy took the opportunity to excuse herself and Frank. They retrieved their coats from the spare bedroom and let themselves out, into the cold night air. Just the two of them on the walking bus back home. Most neighbours were too drunk, with one or two asleep, to notice them leave.
They had survived the evening with their shoes on!

Winter holiday

Yuletide came and went. It had been a wonderful, traditional family Christmas: time spent with the family was always special, it was all about the food and being together. Now they were back home at "Chestnuts", parents returned to their rightful homes, the grandchildren spoilt and their own children happy. What more could they want?

January was always a time to take a break and this year would be no exception. As much as they loved Chestnut Cottage, its new owners had planned a six week cruise to the sun in order to escape the winter chill. They always hoped that on their return, spring would be poking its nose into the garden.

Back in November, as winter had begun to close in at Whisperswood, Daisy decided that a cruise to the sun would be the best cure for any post-Christmas blues that they may find themselves suffering from. Never one to waste time, she had suggested that they head to the Caribbean, the hottest destination at that time of year. Frank never needed any persuasion to go to the sun and they had booked the holiday there and then.

With everything organised and paid for, a couple of months spent sunbathing had been something to look forward to, after the festive season.

There were three cruise ships sailing out of Southampton, that January and the Bests would be leaving on the first of them. They had booked a taxi to pick them up at home and take them directly to the docks, it was easier than driving and not much more expensive than the train, plus, they would have a couple of hours relaxing on the journey Long before reaching the water, they could see their ship, berthed at the terminal in all her pristine glory.

Once onboard ship and having settled into their stateroom, they watched as the majestic vessel slipped anchor, to the sound of a band on the quayside playing and fireworks booming. It was a cold, windy evening and they were glad to be leaving the British winter behind them. Standing together, arms around each other, at the stern of the open promenade deck, Frank thought of the romance that had first brought them together, many years ago and how much he loved Daisy.

The second night on board brought a surprise when, on returning to their cabin, they found a note on the door. As she read the note, Daisy's face creased into a broad smile, she was so surprised. The note was from Bunny and Eric Banks. Unbeknown to either couple, they had both booked the same cruise. The Bankses had spotted them on the deck below, during the sail-away from Southampton but had lost sight before they could meet up. With help from the purser's desk, however, Eric had contrived to have the note to passed on, including a phone number, should they wish to meet for a drink.

Frank lost no time in making the phone call. He spoke to Eric, who was thrilled that the plan had worked. It was entirely possible that they could have spent several days on a ship this size and never run into each other.

The two couples met up for dinner two nights later, in one of the ship's speciality restaurants and it was a fun evening. Having dined together they decided to make a night of it and went dancing, first in the grand ballroom and then in the disco. They laughed all evening; it was a great success. So far, these were still the only people who Frank and Daisy had met in the village, with any real life in them, what a great coincidence that they should be on the ship.

Bunny and Eric were only travelling on the first leg of the voyage and left the ship a few days later as they had a connecting flight to the Bahamas. The four of them spent a couple of hours together at the port, saying goodbyes over a couple of drinks in the sun and promising to meet up on the Bankses' next visit to Whisperswood.

Chapter ten

The Garden Party

The first brave signs of early spring were showing, when the taxi from Southampton pulled up outside Chestnut Cottage. Our sun-bronzed travellers climbed stiffly out of the back seat into the fresh air, just kept from freezing by the bright, low sun, while the taxi driver hefted the luggage out of the boot. He was happy with his generous tip and left a business card in the hope of a repeat booking.

Chestnut Cottage was waiting to welcome them: warm from central heating and filled with the perfume from an enormous bunch of Lilies left in the living room. It was a welcome surprise for two people who had barely seen a cloud in the last ten weeks. They knew straight away that Louise had been round and prepared the house for their return., across one end of the room was pinned a giant sized painting on a length of wallpaper. It featured paint handprints of the children and all the grandchildren, along with various decorations added by the infants, with the title along the top that read: "Welcome Home". 'Oh, we are so lucky.' Daisy cooed. 'Our wonderful grandchildren.' It was good to be home.

Frank and Daisy had returned, renewed in body and spirit, ready to face whatever life could throw at them. Spring soon got into its stride and the garden was picking up nicely. Easter came and went, and they began to settle into life in the cottage, that they had already made so homely. The addition of a luxury summer house in one corner of the garden, encouraged them to spend even more time pruning and clearing the wilderness garden before relaxing al fresco, through the slowly lengthening evenings.

Joan continued to march up and down, with her pack of dogs, alternately pulling her, and she pulling them, as the poor things tired of walking, later in the day. She was still trying to engage anyone she met, with her idle gossip and imagined scandal. Daisy had learned to play her. The Bankses called it "lip service " and regarded it as part and parcel of living in Whisperswood. The aim was to get rid of her as quickly as possible, without letting slip any information that she could rearrange and recycle.

Everyone who went by, remarked on how lovely the garden at Chestnut Cottage, looked, with all her hard work paying off and enquiring how the huge area at the back of the house, was coming on. 'We'd love to come and see it all.' Was such a common remark, that they knew, at some point, they would have to invite all the neighbours round. It would reciprocate the many Christmas drinks invitations.

The days were growing longer and warmer. The garden, although still very much a work in progress, was definitely looking presentable. No one would have believed what it had been like just a year earlier. They had cleared all the way down until it was possible to walk along by the edge of the river, which they discovered, bounded the garden all along one side.

'The house is really too small to entertain more than half a dozen guests.' Frank mused, while they sat outside the summer house, watching trout snapping at flies on the lazy river surface. 'The best part of the property is out here.'

'Why not do something in the garden?' Suggested his wife. 'A "Pimms" and strawberries party; that would be perfect!'

'Yes, great idea! Just the thing. We could fit the whole village in the garden, and we haven't even explored it all yet.' Frank was grinning at the prospect.

With no time to waste, as they sat, drinking their sundowners, Daisy started calculating what supplies they would need while Frank fetched a sheet of paper and commenced the designing of invitations. The date for the party would have to be quite soon, in order to catch the best of the weather, while, at the same time, they would have to give everyone enough notice, to avoid clashes with the date.

So it was, that the next day, they were touring the area on foot, delivering invitations to a summer garden party at Chestnut Cottage. It was a time-consuming job as so many people came out to chat, even though they tried to post the cards without attracting attention. Everyone was enthusiastically accepting the invitation to a new venue and a get together that was not at Christmas.

The day before the garden party, Frank was glued to the weather forecast, which had started out by threatening rain by one o' clock in the afternoon; an hour before the scheduled start time. After two weeks of sunshine, he could not bear the thought of it raining on his "parade". He cheered up later in the day as the forecast changed, bit by bit, until it was wall-to-wall sunshine: Happy days!

As the morning sun began warming the day of the party, and with the weather set fair, it was all systems go in the garden at "Chestnuts".

On the farm, they had used small old-fashioned tin baths for feeding the baby calves. For some reason, a few of them had made their way from the farm to Chestnut Cottage and they proved to be the perfect thing to fill with cold beer, wine, soft drinks and fruit juices. Each of the four tin baths was filled with a selection of beverages, buried in ice cubes.

It did not take long to erect the gazebo and position the various garden tables that they had accumulated over the years. Daisy set one table up with lots of glasses at one end, while at the other end, fresh cut fruit and fresh mint was in the cooler, ready to make the greatest Pimms cocktail, certain to get the party going.

Arranged so that the guests could collect their drink and move straight along, was a second table, set up with strawberries as far as the eye could see. She had strategically placed bowls of snacks and crisps in shaded spots around the garden so that people could nibble as they mingled. The small spare freezer was stocked with ice creams ready for the children.

By late morning, everything was done and the scene was set. Time to relax and have a bite of light lunch, it was going to be a fun afternoon. Two o' clock was to be kick- off.

At one-thirty, Frank opened the drive gates and by two-thirty, the whole place was buzzing, everyone who had an invitation had come, as well as a few people who they did not recognise. That was of no concern, however, as everyone had been told to feel free to invite friends... *Why not?*

Joan made her entrance, the first time they had ever seen her without any dogs and made a bee line straight for Daisy. 'Come on then, give us a tour of your little house.' She had half expected the demand and was resigned to the task, so in they went, closely followed by Gail and Mary Mac.

There was no doubt that the three women were surprised and impressed at the transformation of the old workman's cottage and how nice the couple had made it. Daisy could sense the envy emanating from Joan as she pointed out one improvement after another to her. Gail's eyes were everywhere, as she followed the short tour at Joan's shoulder. Mary Mac. made a few polite remarks but seemed a little vacant; she had perhaps, had a little snifter before arrival.

It did not take long to guide the three judges around the house and, stepping through the back door, they returned to the garden where Joan pronounced her verdict: 'I think you two have done a wonderful job on such an ordinary little house. Anyway, I think we had better try a Pimms now. Come along, Gail' *Was that praise?*

Daisy went to help Frank, who was busy serving glasses of the refreshing cocktail, for all he was worth. Most of the guests were loaded up with strawberries and cream and those who were not, were holding paper plates of savoury nibbles. Everything was going smoothly, with everyone content. Mary Mac. had moved like lightening and was busy knocking back a Pimms, before the rest of the house tour had managed to reach the bar! Within no time, she was absolutely smashed. She had tried a large sample of each wine on offer in between waiting for fresh cocktails to be mixed and delivered to her by various people.

Slightly alarmed at her slurred speech, somebody thoughtfully, sat her in a chair and went for a glass of water. She promptly fell asleep, snoring loudly to the amusement of some and embarrassment of others. Her husband was at a cricket or football match and would be arriving later.

Mr. Jones was enjoying his alcoholic refreshments, along with the odd Pringle that he was dropping down the front of Gail's blouse.… And then trying to retrieve it. She was enjoying the attention and giggling girlishly, as Mr. Big Nose generally ignored her, in fact he was paying a great deal of attention to an extremely curvaceous and much younger woman, who neither Frank nor Daisy recognised and were sure they had not invited. When they asked around, it seemed that no one else had invited her either.

Joan sidled up to Daisy, who was keeping an eye out for anyone without refreshment. 'Another Pimms, Joan?' she offered, holding up a freshly mixed glass jug of the cocktail.

'Oh yes, why not? I am trying to dodge the bores, why on earth did you ask them?' she moaned.

'Because they're all my neighbours!' Daisy replied, indignant at the comment.

'Who, those two?' Joan said indignantly, 'They are MY next door neighbours. Put it this way, I will never get burgled, with that pair next door. They watch everything I do: when I come and when I go. We don't invite them to our parties. Anyway, they don't really have any money.' *Just have a drink and shut up, Joan.*

'Keep your eye on the "Roses" as well. She has been busy digging up the grass verge. Would you believe it, she is growing potatoes on the verge? She has the cheek of the devil.' She spat the accusation out with disgust. 'And if she isn't gardening, she's hanging washing out on her clothesline, haven't you ever noticed it all? Everything is grey.'

Daisy was shocked: 'Are you sure? Who plants potatoes on a verge?' She ignored the comment about the washing.

'Mark my words. Have a look, you can see her potato plants growing between the cow parsley. Wait until September, you'll see her digging them up. Goodness knows what they do with the allotment. Oh yes, I bet you didn't know they've got one of the allotments at the end of the village.' *Another surprise.*

'Please don't let me get caught by Mr. Rose either. He is the most boring man in the world, nothing of any interest to say to anyone. I just don't know what you were thinking, inviting them!' Daisy was at a loss as to what to say in reply to this vindictive onslaught about her neighbours. With her glass refilled, Joan wandered off to gather and spread gossip among the other guests.

Rupert wandered over to the drinks station, it was more than a bar!

'Hello, you two, how goes it? I must say, it was very kind of you to invite me to your little get together.' He was dressed in a very traditional, English, linen summer suit, topped off with a wide brimmed sun hat. As usual, he had his sketch book under one arm while he sipped his iced drink.

'It's going great.' Frank told him. 'And you're very welcome to our party, we wouldn't dream of having one without inviting you!' he added with a grin. Daisy topped up Rupert's drink as they chatted. 'Thank you, sweetie. Now I am going to sit over there in the sun and do a little sketch of the event. Oh, Suzy and James are over there already. I'll have a chat with them while I'm doodling.'

The entire Rose family were present, making the most of the food and drink. Mrs. Rose was talking non-stop, to no one in particular, her husband, nodding in agreement, at her side. He was looking very content, in his unassuming way.

The cake lady, who seemed a good soul, came with her husband, Justin. She was very keen on the cocktails but did not seem bothered what she drank, as long as it kept coming. At one point she was swigging from a bottle of India Pale Ale, while Justin was getting her cocktail topped up for her.

'Please make it a weak one.' He implored Frank, who was in charge of mixing at the time. 'Only she does get a bit carried away.'

he explained, looking around nervously. He was drinking "Seven Up", himself in order to keep a better eye on his wife.

The woman, who talked a lot and thought that grandmas were a bore, was there, talking intently to another guest who was trying to give the impression of listening, just as intently. Her husband, who drank a lot, was sitting comfortably in a wicker garden chair with a small drinks table by his side. He had an impressive selection of beverages on the table and was drinking a lot, as usual.

Everyone had brought their various children, most of whom, were taking instruction from the younger four of the Rose children, down by the river. They were throwing ever bigger sticks and stones into the water, under the sometimes, watchful eye of the eldest Rose, who was perched on a fallen tree trunk and tucking into a plate full of cakes. it was a lovely afternoon.

Daisy had put painted signs up for everything she could think of: For the downstairs cloakroom; a big sign on the ice cream freezer under the gazebo advised: "help yourself" and the same for the drinks. A largely unnecessary, sign, pointed the way to the river.

At about five o'clock, the party had reached its zenith and was showing signs of winding down, when Moaning Mac. arrived to make what he no doubt hoped, would be his grand entrance to the function. Unfortunately for him, despite much loud clearing of his throat and the fact that he was dressed in cricket whites and carrying a cricket bat over one shoulder, nobody noticed him, strutting but at a snail's pace, across the lawn to the now, rather depleted table of strawberries and cakes. Moaning Mac. only ever moved at a sloth-like speed as if his feet were made of lead and it seemed an eternity until he reached his destination.

From his vantage point behind the drinks table, Frank spotted him and went for an interception: 'Hi Moa..' He managed to stop himself from addressing the older man by his common moniker of "Moaning" but realised that he could not remember his real name! Was it Ronald? Feigning a cough, to cover his mistake, he continued:

Hi, Mister MacDonald, glad you could make it.' He lied. 'Can I get you a Pimms?'

'Gin and tonic, please.' The old curmudgeon grunted, without looking at him. Without batting an eyelid, Frank poured a stiff Gordons and Schweppes and handed it to his customer.

'How did the match go?' He asked blithely. 'Humph. So, So.' Was the mumbled answer.

'How many runs did you get?' Cheerfully.

Boxed into a corner and knowing that the scores would be in the local paper next week, Moaning Mac. had to grudgingly admit that he had not actually been playing but was "helping" the umpire. Frank knew nothing about cricket but suspected that the umpire's "helper" could not be all that important.

To close the uneasy conversation, he pointed towards the now peacefully sleeping, Mrs. MacDonald, and said: 'Mary is over there, by the way.' Moaning Mac's face clouded over with anger as he turned to look over to where his wife sat, slumped, head on her chest, in a wicker armchair.

He downed the Gin and tonic in one gulp, hefted the cricket bat as if he was going to hit someone with it, and marched off, slowly, in the direction of his wife.

Now everyone had turned and all eyes were on him. He had achieved his aim but for the wrong reason. Shaking Mary by the shoulder, he whispered through gritted teeth, that it was time for her to leave. Groggily, she rose to her feet and allowed him to steer her, smiling, through the guests, who were parting like the Red Sea, to let them through. Moaning Mac. assured everyone that they would be straight back once he had changed out of his "whites", as they left, steering his wobbling wife through the open gates and out of sight.

After a moment of embarrassed silence, there was a mumble of conversation as neighbours discussed the sudden departure with the general opinion being 'Typical of him'. After another minute, the chatter had returned to normal.

At last, the gathering started to thin out. The MacDonalds bravely returned for 'just one more of those excellent summer cocktails.' Mary's words, she had miraculously gained a second wind. Just the last few guests were still hanging on, reluctant to leave the beautiful setting. It was late in the evening by the time everyone had gone: Job done; a good time had by all.

The hosts set about clearing up the debris; mainly any food waste that might attract the foxes overnight. It had actually been quite hard work but on balance, it had been fun.

As he scooped the left-over strawberries away into a bin bag, Frank said: 'Who did the two teenage girls belong to?'

'I'm not sure, because they all came together. Why?' Daisy asked. He told her that he had seen the girls take a bottle of wine down to the bottom of the garden to drink but had decided not to say anything to upset the apple cart, as everyone was having such a nice time. 'Why did you let them upstairs?'

'I didn't.' she replied, confused. While Franks eyesight was not good, he had seen the two girls at the window of the master bedroom and, as with all people with sight loss, he had very sharp hearing. He said: 'You had best go upstairs and check, because they were in your wardrobe, I heard them open and close the doors.

Daisy dropped the damp cloth that she was cleaning the tables with and ran to the house, straight up the stairs and into the bedroom. There were two fancy antique, headbands; one with pearls and one with feathers, that she kept in an antique narrow vase on the windowsill. They had been thrown on to the bed, the wardrobe door was still open. She looked around, aghast. To one side of the landing, she had a little occasional table on which was displayed an antique fan that she had inherited from her grandmother. The fan had been pulled open so hard that it was ripped in two.

Daisy was heartbroken at the behaviour of these two young girls, who had broken her heirloom. She loved it so much that she couldn't bear to throw it away, which was really the only thing to do with it now. She cursed whichever parent had let their school- age child get drunk on wine, instead of taking the responsibility of watching their child. She was so hurt that anyone would do such a thing but especially the child of a neighbour, to whom she had offered her hospitality.

She knew that her little granddaughter would be just as distraught, to find the damage. She looked at the fan every time she visited her Grandma and knew that it had to be handled very carefully and also that one day it would belong to her.

That was it. They had returned the favour to those whose houses they had been invited to and after that it would never happen again. They found out later, who the girl was, via another neighbour, but they chose to rise above it. What was done was done but these people would not come to the house again. Half of the neighbours had visited, not out of friendship but to assess where the newcomers would fit in, in the social pecking order of Whisperswood.

Chapter eleven

Plans Are Agreed

'Daisy! The phone's ringing!' She dashed through to the front room, that they had fitted out as an office and picked it up. 'Yes, yes, we are here all day.'

'That was a quick phone call.' Frank commented from the top of a step ladder where he was doing his best to dab white paint round a new window frame. She bustled back through from the office, 'Bob and Alison will be here in half an hour. How's that little job going?' He had nearly finished, so the visit would be a nice opportunity for a coffee and a sit down. At last, the architect had the final plans for their extension for them to look at. 'Great!' Daisy got a pot of coffee going, while she prepared a few plates of finger food to offer their friends.

It was several weeks since the garden party and the weather had been wet, with steady rain, for a few days. Bob and Alison parked as close to the front door of "Chestnuts" as possible and ran on tiptoes from the car to the shelter of the little entrance porch. After the hugs and greetings, everyone gathered around the dining table, with the plans spread out for inspection, whilst Bob ran though the details with them. It all seemed to be just what they wanted and included all the alterations that the planning officer had agreed with the architect at an informal meeting.

The planned schedule was to build Frank's new garage first. That would give them some much needed space, they still had things in storage. With the garage built, they could then crack on with the large, open plan, family living space. It was so exciting, it would transform their life: Firstly, he would be able to tinker in his garage once more and hopefully get back to a bit of machine work, with the help of good lighting and a large magnifying glass and of course the family space would enable him to stay on one level, thus avoiding the stairs that he still made a habit of tripping on.

It was agreed, they were all very happy with the plans, Bob had excelled himself in his attention to every detail. The only change they had made to their normal way of working together, was that, for the first time, Frank had engaged a planning consultant. Living in a conservation area and realising the nature of some of the inhabitants of Whisperswood, he was taking no chances in his dealings with the town Council. Bob had agreed that they would forward his plans and sketches to the consultant, who would work his magic on the Council officer responsible for the application. In the past, Frank had always done everything like that. Now as he struggled to regain his independence, his very small contribution would be to walk down to the post box and dispatch the paperwork.

With the important business completed, the four friends relaxed, enjoying each other's company, chatting. The two women left their husbands deep in conversation about nothing in particular and went into the kitchen.

'How's it going with Joan and her bitchy followers?' Alison asked.

'Dreadful. She has made life as difficult as she can, over our plans to extend the house, the gossip always comes back to us one way or another.'

'Don't worry, Bob submits plans every day and every day, he meets jealous neighbours. It will pass, don't give up on what you want to do because of her. You and Frank have both been through so much in the past couple of years.'

'I know. I try to shield him but some days, I just cannot face another nasty neighbour. What I don't get, is that "Chestnuts" is the only cottage in Whisperswood, that has never been extended.'

'Look.' Said Alison. when you bought this place, it was a tip! and I mean a real tip: Derelict, as near as damn it; rats and mice running around, not fit to live in. It has lain empty for years, it's where the poor people lived and in the neighbours' minds, it still is.

'Now look! You pair have come along, the ground has been cleared to reveal the most amazing views across the valley, the overgrown, collapsed hedge has been cut and shaped, the lawns are sweeping and I bet no one knew that the river was even there, you couldn't see it.

'Daryl has made great progress upstairs; the bathrooms are beautiful, the curtains so soft and luxurious. Oh yes and the rats are gone! But not far hey?' She said, with a jerk of her head towards the road leading to Mrs. Lupus's lair. 'And the subservient people that lived here have long gone. They are jealous, Daisy!

'Nobody complained when it was lying in a state of neglect; empty, rats running around, with weeds growing out of the roof. Oh, but they are now! That it might just end up better than theirs, ha! They're….' She struggled to find a word strong enough, 'prats!' Alison squealed with frustrated anger. Daisy was shocked at her friend's outburst; she had never seen her so wound up.

They wandered back to rejoin their men who were now at the front door. 'Bob always says he could write a book about neighbours, with their nastiness. Jealous people, that never act alone, always part of a gang, causing misery. They bring out the dark side of humanity. You will come out of this with your dignity and of course, victorious. Remember, they are all very weak, alone, that's why they are in a gang. Empty, bored people, struggling with the fear that somebody else might have something they don't.

'Look, we have eaten all your food. We must go, we have one more set of plans to drop off to a client. We'll see you on Friday, you are still coming for dinner, aren't you?'

'Yes, of course.' said Daisy. 'Wouldn't miss it for the world.'

'Okay, I will cook for seven.' Alison gave both her friends each a peck on the cheek and slipped her hand through Bob's arm as he opened the door. With a cheery wave, they tip-toed back over the wet grass and hopped into their car, driving sedately away, out of Whisperswood to their next appointment.

Nasty Neighbours

Frank walked to the post box to send the amended building plans to Mr. Dunn, the planning consultant. It had taken a lot longer than anticipated but between hospital visits, things had had to wait. On route, he met Rupert, whose face lit up on seeing him. 'Hello, old chap, how are you getting on? He asked in his cut glass accent.

'I'm very well, thanks. Yourself?'

'Oh, marvellous, as always. I was just walking down to see you, I wanted to give you this.' He handed Frank a large package, wrapped in brown paper and tied with string, in a very old-fashioned way.

'What is it?' He asked.

'When I came to "Chestnuts" for the lovely garden party you threw, I created a little doodle of the event, against the backdrop of the house. I've framed the drawing, please enjoy it.' He spoke in a very self-facing manner which belied his considerable artistic talent.

'Thank you so much,' Frank said, delighted. 'what a kind thought. I know Daisy will be thrilled with it.'

'You're very welcome. It's not much, but it's just a little thank you. I shan't stop, I have one of my students waiting.' he continued, and with another, 'Thank you', left Frank to his task. The narrow road was awash with rainwater and the pillar box was sitting in a small, water-filled moat, which called for a long reach in order to deposit the envelope safely through the letter slot whilst keeping one's feet dry.

Hurrying home, with Rupert's package under his coat to protect it from the rain, He had a strange encounter. Seeing a car coming towards him from the opposite direction, he stopped to wait on the narrow, grass verge, while it passed. As the vehicle approached, it sped up, ploughing through a deep puddle, saturating the pedestrian from his feet to his chest. He recognised the unmistakable profile of Mr. Big Nose at the wheel, staring intently ahead as he passed, showing no recognition of his victim.

As he squelched back into the house, Daisy remarked that the rain 'must have been heavier than you expected, Frank!' But her lighthearted expression changed to puzzlement as he explained how

Big Nose had made a deliberate effort and succeeded! to soak him. Why would he do such a thing?

'Forget that, though. I met Rupert and he gave me this.', he produced the slightly damp package from his open coat and passed it to his wife who took it into the kitchen to unwrap on the worktop. The incident with Big Nose was forgotten and she let out a gasp of surprise as the wrapping opened up to reveal a stunning pencil drawing, tinted with pale watercolour tints. Against the backdrop of Chestnut Cottage, the garden party was depicted in luxurious detail, with figures enjoying the event, the gazebos, even the bowls of strawberries. Daisy felt as if she could step into the picture, so lifelike was it.

The small gift made her feel so happy. It was a beautiful, thoughtful gift from a kind neighbour, which Rupert, indeed, was.

After his unpleasant encounter with the big nosed neighbour, Frank gave up walking alone, completely. With his reduced vision, they were both afraid that he may get run over by accident, if not design. A few days later, as they were walking together, near the cottage, they had another shock as Big Nose once again, sped by, dangerously close to them. So, the first time was no accident. The aggressive driver had a problem with both of them but they were at a loss as to what it could be.

Frank reasoned that the last time they had seen him had been at their home when they had hosted the drinks in the garden. He had come along with Gail although the relationship had struck him as odd: His obsession with the other woman and neither of them bothering about Mr. "Wandering hands" Jones doing his lost crisp trick down the female Big Nose's modest cleavage.

They knew very little about him, except that on the two occasions that he had spoken to Frank, it had been all about trying to impress. Joan didn't like him, although she did not like most people, but whenever she mentioned him, she always included "big headed" and "know-all" in the same sentence.

It's strange moving to an area where everyone has known everyone for a long time, a new arrival can upset the equilibrium. Maybe he felt threatened by the new arrivals: successful, effortlessly attractive and popular.

Daisy couldn't help but suspect that Joan was behind it all. Poor, big nosed, Gail, who hardly had model looks herself, had confided in Joan about her husband and the babysitter. The secret had gone around the village like wildfire, with everyone sniggering behind the hapless Mrs. Big Nose's back.

At first, Joan had only given the sordid details to a "few" chosen acquaintances but once Mary Mac. heard the news, the tale grew legs and now it was public knowledge to everyone. Naturally, each time the story was repeated it grew more salacious.

Surely' people are the same the world over? They all want to live in a nice environment, love their family, they want them to be safe, happy and healthy. Something was wrong, here in whispers wood, where these values did not seem to count.

Chapter twelve

Council Workmen at Whisperswood

The long hot summer was now well and truly ended, the grandchildren were back at school and autumn had arrived. Chestnut Cottage's garden was now under control with new blossom trees and evergreen shrubs planted in readiness for the following year. The evergreens would create privacy and wind breaks for the summer roses that were set out everywhere.

This once, near-derelict cottage, unloved for years, had been transformed and was now the prettiest of the pretty little row of cottages in the village… and they had not yet finished working their magic on it.

Daisy went out into the front garden, armed with a trowel and a large bag of mixed bulbs. Her intention was to underplant the lawn with daffodils and tulips, ready for next spring. From further along the road, came the din of a very noisy machine, it sounded like a tractor with a hedge cutter. As she glanced down the lane in the direction of the noise, she saw Mrs. Lupus walking towards her.

The old woman offered no greeting; simply launching into a tirade, starting with: 'Oh it's you, Maisy.' Daisy had corrected her before, but the old crone was still either deaf or just too belligerent to say her name properly. 'The Council are here; they have come to cut my hedge back. I can't see anything wrong with it, can you?' Before Daisy could answer, she continued: 'It's only my hedge that keeps the traffic down. You just see! If they cut it back now, the road will be full of commuters by tomorrow! This is only supposed to be a goat track. I have so many letters from the Parish Council about my hedge that I never need to buy toilet paper!' *What a vile old bat!*

The sound of machinery stopped and three burly men, dressed in bright orange, Council overalls, strolled up, casually inspecting the huge hedge. They all waved a friendly hello at Daisy as they approached but pointedly ignored the person responsible for their presence in the road.

'Are you alright, Mrs. Lupus, have you spoken to them?' She asked quietly. It seemed the neighbourly thing to do, to check that her elderly neighbour understood what was happening and was comfortable with the presence of the work gang and their equipment. She need not have worried; Lupus was more than a match for anyone that the Council could send.

'I'm alright! Why shouldn't I be?' she demanded rudely. 'We have agreed on two foot. That will take it back to my garden and away from the road. I am going to stand and watch them. Make sure they do it properly!'

'Well, as long as you're happy with that.'

'Yes. Of course I am. I knew it would be cut eventually but it does make the traffic slow down. It will soon grow back…faster than they can get organised to come back and chop it again.', she declared, jerking a thumb in the direction of the Council truck.

She stood and watched Daisy begin planting her bulbs, whilst dispensing unsolicited advice to "Maisy", on how deep she should plant them, when to prune roses and how to garden, generally, until one of the workmen started a chainsaw up. Upon hearing the engine's ear-splitting whine, she whirled around as if on a parade ground, and marched off to check on what was happening.

After three or four hours, the noise of cutters and strimmers petered out. Two of the Council workmen began to load the truck with all the hedge clippings and lengths of small tree that they had chopped. The other fellow swept the road clear of the larger pieces of debris.

My, Daisy thought to herself, *that looks like a great job.*

The workmen, their job finished, retreated to their truck, for a smoke and a cup of tea. They had been working hard nearly all morning.

Mrs. Lupus reappeared in the lane to survey the results. She made a show of satisfaction as she made her way, clumping along in her lace-less, men's shoes, straight to "Chestnuts". 'Oh, I am glad I decided to get the hedge cut back now, it looks so much better.' Daisy remained supportive towards her whilst the workmen were there; *after all,* she thought, *she is a very elderly lady, all be it a cantankerous one.* But the way that she had claimed the enforced maintenance as her own idea, left Daisy stunned at the old woman's arrogance. After so much to-ing and fro-ing, there had been no choice; the council were going to chop her hedge, one way or another. And now at last, they had. The improvement was drastic and well worth the effort; there really was a road, no longer, a single-track lane.

When Frank came home later that day, he was surprised and thrilled at the transformation of the narrow lane he had left that morning into a clear, single lane road. He was even more surprised when he heard the account of the morning's visit by the council's enforcement team and that Mrs. Lupus had taken their activities so calmly but Daisy thought that she had seemed, somehow, relieved that the hedge was finally cut back out of the way. 'Perhaps it was all getting a bit overwhelming for her.' She still felt that the rude old woman should be given the benefit of the doubt, because of her age. Frank reminded her that, 'Just because nasty people grow old, it doesn't mean they aren't still nasty.'

The battle over Mrs. Lupus' hedge had been going on long before the Bests had moved to Whisperswood. When they had gone walking, they had noticed her putting all sorts of things along the edge of the road: There were lots of bricks, large stones, lengths of barbed wire, lumps of wood, even a broken TV. Aerial, to force the traffic away from the hedge and discourage people from driving along the road at all.

Joan had once asked Daisy if she had seen her putting the obstacles out. Sometimes, she would stack them one on top of the other, they were always amazed that she could lift the heavier pieces. The gossip had warned her: 'Don't come out walking at nine o'clock in the evening, you will bump into Moaning Mac. It drives him crazy, so, at night, he comes down and picks it all up and throws it away.' Lowering her voice, she had added: 'I have to confess, I do as well but please don't tell her, will you?'

Well, now there would be no need for bricks and lumps of wood. The hedge was cut, and the rubbish removed. Motor traffic could traverse the road safely again without the risk of hitting dangerous pieces of junk along the edge. The fight over Mrs. Lupus and her overgrown hedge was finished, For now.

Who could that be knocking at this time of the morning? Daisy opened the door to find Joan standing there, dogs milling around as far their leads would allow, behind her.
'Are you coming for coffee at Mrs. Lupus's this morning?'
'No, sorry.' *They won't take "no" for an answer.* 'It is my day at the hospital voluntary service. My friend will be here shortly, to pick me up. Joan was ready for a chat but Daisy could hardly invite her in, she would be stuck with her all morning, or until she left to meet Lupus, for coffee.
'Anyway,' the toxic visitor began gossiping straightaway: 'Have you seen the mess in Justin's garden? That's the one next door to Mrs. Lupus.' He has had one of those little diggers in there to change everything around but he was driving it himself, he hasn't a clue what he's doing. It is such a mess, you would think a child had been in there doing it, it's so hideous and the worst part is they keep wanting to show it off to everybody because they are so proud of it!' she snorted. Daisy had only ever heard Joan laugh in a Schadenfreude manner, never simply because something was funny, she did not have a normal sense of humour.
Daisy was sure the house in question, was where the cake lady, who seemed a good soul, lived. Was there no end to this woman's meanness? She repeated her apology regarding morning coffee and with, 'I really must get ready to go out, see you later.' wished Joan a good day and shut the door. Relaxing with her back leaning against it, she breathed a sigh of relief. She thought of her mother who always said: 'People who love themselves, don't hurt others.' but this woman was hurting her neighbours by the bucket load. She clearly was unfulfilled in her marriage, her life was dogs and gin, perhaps not what she had hoped for.

The "toot-toot" of a car horn, announced Daisy's lift arriving outside. Time to go. 'Frank! Jenny's here, I'm off.' She dashed out of the house and jumped in her friend's car and they took off up the road, chatting, laughing and of course, exchanging funny stories about their young grandchildren.

Jenny was a slim, attractive woman, with lovely long blonde hair. She wore it with gold extensions but when it was pinned up on top of her head, she still looked like a nurse. Daisy always used to say to Frank: 'If ever I am ill, get Jenny.' She was the sweetest, kindest person you would want around you if you were ill. She was what the NHS now lacked; a kind, caring soul, full of compassion and empathy.

Daisy had to break it to her that this would be the last week she would go to the hospital as she no longer felt she could leave Frank at home, alone.

Her great friend was upset at the news but understood; family had to come first. They had enjoyed many great times over the years and their long friendship was something they had both cherished and knew it would continue. They would both always be there for each other, with their ups and downs in life, with the children and of course, the unstoppable passion they each had for their grandchildren, the love for their husbands and the mutual respect they had for each other.

Daisy had told Jenny about her dreadful neighbours. Unfortunately, she had her own set of bad guys, with parking wars and noisy children. it seemed that everyone she spoke to, had a beef with their neighbour.

Even the Best's accountant, the mildest mannered, easiest going fellow one could meet, had experienced a problem with his neighbours. He had converted his garage, to create an extra bedroom and the neighbour objected because she didn't want to live next door to building works. Her complaint was that she had lived in London for many years where everyone was always building, so she had moved to the country for peace and quiet only to find the same thing happening next door. Her own house had already had the garage converted. Unbelievably selfish but everyone, it seemed, was living with the bad taste of unfriendly neighbours

The Bankses were over for a few days, staying in their holiday home and Bunny phoned to say that she had picked up four tickets for a charity dinner in town. Naturally, the call ended with an invitation to 'come and have a coffee and we can catch up.'

It was a quiet day for Frank and Daisy; for once, they had no tradesmen at the cottage and no pressing renovation jobs to do. The weather was exceptionally mild, so they left what they were doing, no need for coats and set off walking, to meet their friends for a chinwag. It wasn't really far enough to bother going by car and it was always nice to taste the clean, fresh, country air.

As they reached the entrance to Mrs. Lupus's house, they met Gail, being dragged along by the brown Labrador. She had just left the daily coffee morning, strangely, without Joan.

They politely greeted her with a 'good morning' and kept walking but she was clearly very agitated and managed to haul the panting dog to a halt: 'Do you know, what those Council men did to Mrs. Lupus was really mean!' She blurted out in a whingeing voice. The couple stopped and turned to look at the ridiculous woman, dressed head to toe in her country tweed and waxed cotton. *Does she never get hot?*

'What did they do?' Daisy asked, for a moment, genuinely concerned for the old woman.

'Fancy chopping an old lady's hedge back like that. She is so upset!' Mrs. Big Nose had worked herself up into a childlike anger at the perceived injustice. *Firstly, it was your friend, Joan, who had tirelessly campaigned to get it chopped back. And secondly, Mrs. Lupus had agreed with the council men how much they would cut back.*

'Oh, I don't know about that.' she replied tactfully, 'I think it's a big improvement, don't you?'

'Well it will be easier for me to drive through…' She was a little calmer now. They were able to leave the conversation at that and carry on their way, as the Labrador fortuitously lunged at a leaf, blowing across the road and pulled Gail away in the opposite direction.

Bunny and Eric had noticed the difference made by the Council's efforts as soon as they arrived, by car, in Whisperswood. It was the first thing they remarked on, after greeting their friends. Everyone was entertained over coffee with the story of the visit by the Council workmen, Old Mother Lupus's carry on about what they could do and lastly whatever yarn she had spun to the impressionable Mrs. Big Nose.

Chapter thirteen

Trouble

Frank was back in hospital for more complex eye surgery, in mid-December, meaning a stay there of several days. It meant extra stress for Daisy and the ward staff had kindly relaxed the visiting rules for her, because her husband was so ill. she was there nearly all day, helping to care for him, only coming home to sleep at the end of evening visiting time.

With the operation declared a partial success, he was released to the care of his wife, only because she was a trained nurse and would be able to continue the post operation care needed. It was nearly Christmas again but this time he was slower to recover. He found being out on his own difficult and he was relying more than ever on her to help him through the day. Sometimes, it felt as if they took one step forward, followed by two steps backwards.

There were far more important things on Daisy's mind than opening the post that had gathered in the hallway while Frank had been in hospital. Now he was back and sitting in front of the fire, relaxing, she found time to sit down herself and go through the mail. It was mostly Christmas cards from their many friends scattered around the country and, indeed, various parts of the world. Amongst the envelopes, was a Christmas drinks invitation from the Joneses. It had been two nights ago, so they had missed it. *Phew! What a relief.* But it meant that there were probably five more to come!

They tried to continue with daily walks. The exercise was good for them both and it helped with Frank's recovery and for his eyes to cope with light sensitivity. They began to notice that they were getting the cold shoulder from a couple of people. At first, they brushed it off as coincidence but as the days went by, they both began to feel uncomfortable whenever they came across one of Joan's clique of associates, the same ones that had pestered them to socialise when they had arrived in the village. Something was wrong and they had no idea what had caused the change.

They kept themselves to themselves for a while, which was the way they liked it, until one morning, on the way back from their walk. Daisy could see Joan in the distance, she was almost galloping down the road like a bolting horse, to catch them up, pulling all her various dogs behind her for all she was worth. They paused and turned to watch the spectacle; she was waving her free hand at them now. The gossip was so fit due to the time spent walking her dogs, that when she reached them, she was hardly panting.

'Right, You two, I want a word!' Her aggression took them by surprise.

'I beg your pardon.' Frank said quietly.

'if you two want to live around here you have to get on with us. What's wrong with you?' she demanded. 'Nothing.' He replied. 'Well, you did not attend the drinks and you refuse invitations. That is not the way we work here in Whisperswood.'

'Well,' he said, 'we have had a few things on.' not wanting to discuss his latest surgery.

'Well anyway, we have all had a chat about you.'

'I am sure you have.' He answered.' 'That's what you do, Joan: Gossip.' His wife pulled him by the elbow. 'Come on, let's go. This isn't what we do.' He relented and taking her lead, turned to follow her away from the outraged Joan.

As they walked away, shocked at the outburst, the gossip stood and watched, furious that they should turn their back on her. She continued calling after them as she stood, impotent in her fury, surrounded by panting dogs that were also ignoring her.

A car came slowly around the corner, it was the husband of the cake lady, who seemed like a good soul. Joan flagged him down, a look of triumph on her face. 'Run along.' she shouted at the departing couple. 'We are just going to have a nice gossip about you!' They both shook their head in disbelief. This was the man who, according to Joan, had the digger in his "hideous garden making child's play." Now she was gossiping to him about them. They returned home, so upset at what had happened. If She wasn't mad, this woman was evil. *Who on earth did she think she was? "If you want to live here."* But what was the problem? They had put up with this woman from the day after they had moved to the village. Perhaps that was their mistake; ever speaking to her in the first place.

No more invites came for Christmas drinks, they were so relieved but also knew that there was a reason behind it. Frank had suspected for some time that Joan was behind the problem as she was behind most unpleasantness that happened in Whisperswood.

There was still time to fit an overdue trip to London in before Christmas and between medical appointments, so they arranged for the whole extended family to meet in the West end for a slap-up meal and the theatre. Nobody really minded which production they saw but of course, the grandchildren were begging to see a pantomime. It took a lot of searching to find somewhere with enough seats left but with the most expensive seats to watch Disney's "Aladdin", costing an arm and a leg, there were sure to be plenty unsold. The Best family filled most of them and everyone declared it a worthwhile expense.

The younger Bests stayed in London that night and returned home the next morning, leaving the old ones to enjoy a couple of days in the Capital, simply taking in a more mature theatre production, a couple of nice meals at landmark restaurants and the pre-Christmas hustle and bustle

Rupert was out and about, delivering his Christmas cards. He gave a polite, rat-a-tat, on Chestnut Cottage's front door knocker.

'Hello, Rupert, come in.' Frank greeted him. In the short time they had lived at "Chestnuts", Rupert had always been very pleasant to them, as he was to everyone. He clearly still missed his partner: 'He was my everything.' he confided in Frank. 'When I walk up the lane, I feel my arm is missing. To write the Christmas cards is so very hard, just writing my own name, no other. I always keep the radio on, up at the cottage, it's the quietness, I find so hard to bear.'

'You can come up here to us, anytime you like.' Daisy assured him as she joined the two men in the sitting room.

'You're very kind.' Rupert replied with a moistening eye. My painting classes keep me busy and I have to say, happy, most of the time. How are you settling in? It can take years in a village like this.'

'Well, we love being here and of course, being so near to the family, is wonderful. I must say, we find Joan a little strange.' he said delicately, aware that Rupert was a gentle soul. 'Ah. Yes, Joan.' Rupert spoke slowly, as if choosing his words. 'She has a drink problem. Used to be an average sort of woman...well, not quite the sociopath she is now, but I'm afraid she has caused a lot of upset in the village. Be careful. My lovely Tom had a saying: "There is nothing more important than being kind." I try to live my life like that every day.' He stood up to leave. 'I'm so sorry I can't stay a little longer but I really must beat the postman to the post box, he'll be emptying it soon.'

'You are the sweetest person, Rupert. We wish you a wonderful Christmas.' Daisy gave him a hug and kissed him on the cheek, which he returned, with a smile.

The planning consultant, Mr. Dunn, had been recommended by a friend in "the know". It was common knowledge that he had never lost an application, with three different County Councils and he was just the man they needed. He had arranged a site meeting with the council planning officer at Chestnuts Cottage, just before Christmas and the official had poured over the proposed plans, changed a few ground rules; what they could and could not do, as far as design and materials and made one or two suggestions of things she would 'prefer to see in the design'. The consultant knew that she would do this, to exert her position of power. He also knew exactly how to handle her and get everything he wanted. He was totally confident as he went off to tweak the plans. He was a clever chap, whose confidence was well founded and his latest clients had complete faith in him.

Frank was not well enough to travel in January, so they resolved to stay in England this winter. It would be their first January spent in England, for twenty years: they always went off in search of some sunshine but as there were myriad things to prepare and tradesmen to schedule, it was probably for the best, that they would be at home. Regarding the start date, actually breaking ground, they would have to wait for a decision from the planning authority.

He so wanted to have his garage built and the house extension was designed to enable him to live downstairs. Removing the stairs from the equation of his life, would make a huge difference. It would enhance not only his own but also his wife's life, it would mean less of her husband's accidents to cope with!

The Gang Up

Daisy began to notice Joan; sometimes alone, at other times with various people who she did not recognise, standing near Chestnut Cottage with cameras and papers in hand, pointing in various directions over the cottage's very large garden, the garden that had shocked everyone with its size, including the owners, when the dilapidated, long boundary markers had finally been discovered.

It was clear that the viewers were trying to work out where the proposed building would be. This went on day after day. She would walk up and down with her dogs in the morning, trying to peer over the hedge. Most afternoons, she would reappear, without half of the dogs, because they were so unruly, and carrying tatty plastic bags, bulging with papers. This time she was door knocking, canvassing support for her campaign to prevent the Bests' proposed building works. She seemed all too powerful, it was as if she had a hold over everyone in her drinking/dinner party, circle. Her forceful personality and policy of divide and conquer, meant that she was the only one to communicate with everybody, consequently, her word was gospel. If you chose to say otherwise, you would be out of the clique and in the wilderness.

On this particular day, the campaigning troublemaker was standing just along the road from "Chestnuts", with Jane, explaining the need for her to join her crusade. Jane always wore a fixed, patronising smile on her face which belied her self-serving, determined nature.

Frank glanced out of the office window and spotting the two women, remarked to Daisy: 'The way I see it is: Joan's the bully and they are all afraid of being left out, so they just go along with what she says. The other option is to become her next victim. It seems to me that all her little gang are stuck in shallow friendships.'

Eventually, the time limit was reached for any objections to the proposed works at Chestnut Cottage and the Council Planning Department made their decision. Mr. Dunn sent a letter addressed to Mr. & Mrs. Best. In it he explained that although the planning officer had no problem with the application per se, enough local people had written letters of objection to the proposal that there would have to be a full meeting before a ruling could be made. He went on to say that it had obviously been a "gang up" and that they had somehow nobbled the local Councillor who had come onboard with the objectors.

In summary, the planning permission had been refused, not because the plans were at fault and not because the planners did not like them. The rules said that a certain number of written objections, forced an application to be heard at a planning committee meeting. It was simply because of a bunch of bullies on a power trip.

Now they had confirmation of what they already knew: Joan had been stirring up trouble. All the letters of objection to their plans had been written by her cronies, some of whom, were on the parish council and, even worse, they all followed the same template! Presumably supplied by her.

Frank finished reading the letter and let it fall on the kitchen table. 'Well, old girl, they all came here and accepted our hospitality; we know they all stab each other in the back, why are we surprised that they should do it to us as well? Do you realise that each one of these letter writers lives in an extended house?' In fact, Chestnut

Cottage was the only dwelling in Whisperswood that had not been enlarged at some point in its history.

He could not comprehend why these people were not at home enjoying their life, when instead, they chose to spend their time preventing someone else from living theirs.

'We have two choices now, love: give up and keep the cottage as it is, or fight the decision, which means fighting that sad old bitch and her cronies.'

'So that's decided then. You had better ring Mr. Dunn.'

Mr. Dunn was not fazed by the initial refusal of permission by the town planners, it was all grist to the mill for him, he thrived on the challenge....and made more money in the process.

'It's well known, Mister Best,' he intoned, 'that local parish councils are generally made up of oddballs, bullies and idiots, with nothing or very little, going on in their lives. They are usually retirees, who dislike change, unless it is to their own advantage and come in various degrees of shall we say? social mobility. One has to ask what would induce someone to become a parish councillor where the biggest challenge might be to keep the grass cut in the churchyard?'

Most of them are just witches' covens of trouble-making gossips. Their opinion counts for nothing with the town council and nobody's going to listen to it, regarding your planning application. The best thing you can do now is forget about it. Just leave it to me, I will let you know when the appeal hearing is.'

Frank put the receiver down, surprised at Mr. Dunn's vehement dislike of parish councils and their members and more so, that he would share it with a client. He did, however, have to admit that he agreed with everything that the consultant had said.

Many things in life are affected by the input from various authorities and individuals who wield a small amount of power or influence. This power will always be open to abuse and parish councils are a prime example. The parish councillors were abusing their power, such as it was and, at Joan's behest of Joan's, were effectively, bullying the Bests. The saying that power should never be granted to those who crave it is very true. These people craved power and now the Bests were about challenge it.

Frank gave a little chuckle that prompted his wife to give him a questioning look. In response he recounted a story he had heard a few weeks before from their friend, Bernie. He owned a very popular pub, "The Plasterers Trowel", in a nearby village. It was the sort of place where you had to book a table a week in advance if you wanted to eat there.

The story went that Bernie had been ill: He had broken his foot a year before and although it had healed, he was now having difficulty walking. He went to his doctor's surgery and asked the receptionist for an appointment to see the doctor. 'Is it an emergency?' she asked.

'Well, no but I would like to see someone.' After all, he had to earn a living and was on his feet all day.

'I'm afraid, we have nothing for two weeks.' she told him, coldly. 'I have just the one appointment, take it or leave it. She was wielding her little piece of power. What could the patient do but hobble back home and wait for two weeks?

As it happened, later that week, Bernie was busy at his bar on a Sunday lunchtime and the pub was buzzing with the conversation of happy customers. If you wanted good food it was the best place for miles around, always chockablock. He was always happy to serve a drink at the bar whilst patrons sat and waited for a table.

Who should walk in desperately searching for a table? While she had no reason to remember Bernie, he was just one of dozens of people she saw every day, he certainly remembered her: it was the unhelpful doctor's receptionist. Putting on her best pleading smile, she asked: 'Do you have a table for four please?'

'Do you have a table booked?' The proverbial tables were well and truly turned. 'No.' she replied, 'I thought you might be able to squeeze us in.'

'No. Can't do that.' he told her. 'I can take a reservation for two weeks' time.' As the crestfallen woman turned away from the bar, one of Bernie's regulars, who had heard the exchange and also recognised her, cheerfully chirped from his bar stool: 'Now you know what it feels like, love!'

As Bernie concluded his tale, he had said to Frank: 'Do you know how good that felt? All week, her word is final but, on a Sunday, in my pub, MY word is final!
The story made them both laugh, it was real karma.

Behind the pretty stone cottages and country gardens, Whisperswood had a similar social mix to any other village. Not everyone was well-heeled and living the countryside dream. As well as the big houses, there were the tenanted homes, many of which, housed families living on the minimum wage. There were the lonely folk; the bereaved and then there were the new people like the Bests.

The clique of bullies may have thought that they ran the village with their monopoly of the parish council and deciding who went to whose dinner parties but actually it was a village of two unequal halves. Most of its inhabitants had nothing to do with Joan, or the Joneses for that matter. They were not bothered who had lived there the longest or whose house was better than the next.
When they were out and about, Frank and Daisy would often bump into Rupert or see him waving from his garden, lost in his world of painting. There were Suzy and James, strolling by with their baby granddaughter in the pushchair, who always stopped for a natter; or Bunny Banks shouting from the window: 'Come and have a jar!' Of course, there was always the sound of the gate opening as a loved family member came to visit. They had a lot to be thankful for.

As the weeks ticked by towards the date of the Planning appeal, Frank and Daisy found themselves sent to Coventry by the same people who had smothered them with visits and invitations during the first year at Whisperswood. Each time they left the house, they ran the gauntlet of meeting one of Joan's associates.
Locals were peering in at "Chestnuts" at every opportunity, in the hope of seeing some sign of building works that they could discuss with each other. Daisy even saw the old man who drank a lot,

the one married to the woman who talked a lot, standing in his garden, blatantly watching them through a large pair of binoculars, while she played with the grandchildren in the garden. It was simply terrible, what on earth did he think he would achieve?

Gail had taken to peering through the garden hedge at the front of the house, poking her phone through to take photos of the garden. She was ever desperate to impress Joan so it would be a feather in her cap if she could be the first to show her idol, evidence of building work.

It became apparent that several households in Whisperswood had been the victims of the same gang of bullies in the past. There was even a "Good luck" card posted through the door from a supporter who felt the need to remain anonymous.

Frank suggested a break from the claustrophobic atmosphere of the village until the date of the planning appeal meeting. It seemed a good idea, so they upped sticks and moved into Christmas Cottage for a few weeks where they were once again surrounded by true friends and kindness. It was like being on holiday and when the time came, they were sorry to leave but they had to face reality and the big day was almost upon them.

The day after returning home, they had a call from Frank's eye surgeon who was travelling back to London. He knew his patient well, as his injuries and complications were unusual and he had let many students observe his treatment as part of a research programme. He was going to be passing close by on his journey and would like to call in to see how things were progressing. He would be giving a lecture in London and wanted a couple of photos 'just as visual aids, pardon the pun!' which he could take himself.

Of course, they were more than happy to accommodate him after all the extra time and effort he had spent on the case. Having given him directions to the house, Daisy told him that she would stand outside, giving directions by phone and wave, once she saw him in the lane. It was an awkward address to find through the narrow country roads.   She was standing by the newly installed drive gates, talking to the surgeon, on the phone, when she noticed both the Big Noses walking along the lane towards her. Gail was struggling to control the brown Labrador as always, while the male Big Nose minced along beside her, hands in the pockets of his Barbour jacket. They were arguing furiously, shouting at each other, apparently oblivious to the unwilling witness.

Daisy realised with a groan, that it must be time for coffee with Mrs. Lupus and Big Nose (male) was off work, so had to attend as well. As they drew level with her, the arguing ceased abruptly, replaced by an embarrassed silence. Gail ignored Daisy and stayed on course for the Lupus residence, bouncing along behind the panting dog. Not so her husband.

Deciding that he could not ignore their audience as if nothing had happened, he raised a limp hand to smooth his floppy hair and, leaving Gail to carry on, he swaggered up to Daisy: 'Ha! You won't get your planning; we will stop you. it's not fair, we all had to jump through hoops for our planning and so can you! You're new round here, you'll have to learn how things are done.'

Gail began shouting at him again but now, she wanted him to catch up with her in case they should miss anything at Lupus's. 'Shut up, Gail!' He yelled back at her.

'Go away right now.' Daisy quietly ordered him. She thought: *Not now please. The doctor is going to come around the corner any minute, how embarrassing.*

Gail began to lose all control and started screaming at the male Big Nose; 'Come here! Come here! Don't talk to her, don't talk her.' She was apoplectic as she screamed at the top of her voice: 'If you don't come here right now, you big nosed bastard, I am going to kill you!'

The noise was so intense in the quiet of the countryside that it had aroused the ever-vigilant Mary Mac, who now appeared at a safe distance. 'I say, Gail. Do keep it down, you sound like a fishwife. Go home if you are going to fight with him. Please, not in the street.'

'It's not a street, it's a country lane, you gin soaked old cow.' Gail shouted back, tears streaming down her face, as she rounded on Mary MacDonald, who staggered back in shock at the verbal abuse. Gail had always seemed so demure and friendly in her immature way.

With all eyes now on Mary Mac., who looked as if she was about have a heart attack, Big Nose took his opportunity to turn away from Daisy and quickly minced / swaggered as best he could, to join his red faced wife who's temper was coming down from explosive to boiling.

This was way out of control. The Big Noses disappeared behind Mrs. Lupus's tall garden gate, just as the consultant's car appeared at the far end of the road. He spotted Daisy straightaway and pulled smartly up, past her into the gravel driveway behind the open gates.

For a portly gentleman in his sixties, the surgeon was surprisingly agile and had leapt out of the driver's seat before Daisy had followed him into the driveway. He shook her hand and enquired: 'My dear Mrs. Best, are you alright?'

'Yes, yes, I am fine, thank you.'

'Who was the lunatic screaming?' He asked with a puzzled frown. I could hear it all on the phone.' He was very shocked indeed, 'It's not every day you hear that sort of carry-on over the phone.'

'It's a long story, I'm afraid.' she explained, sadly, then changing the subject: 'Come on in. Frank is waiting for you, he's not too good today I'm afraid.'

The surgeon gave his patient a quick, unofficial checkup and pronounced him to be recovering slower than expected but somewhat depressed. He pressed Daisy again about the "carry-on" he had heard on the phone and she explained everything that had gone on.

She decided that the easiest thing would be to play the whole scene back on the CCTV for him to see. The camera, high on the front of chestnut cottage, had captured everything. He was so shocked that he sat in silence throughout the few minutes it took to watch it.

Quietly but determinedly, he said: 'You cannot live like this because of a planning application, we must phone the police. This is way too stressful for Frank's health, not to mention your own. This is not normal living, that woman needs arresting. It is an offence to scream and shout like that at someone in the street, I should think it comes under "breach of the peace." Either way, if you call the police, I will speak to them on your behalf.

It was the strangest medical consultation that anyone could experience. They were touched by the surgeon's kindness, could not believe it. The great man had shown that just because he was a busy, important man at the top of his profession, it did not mean that he was not human.

They tried to put it all out of their minds, reasoning, as anybody might, that once the planning was approved it would all die down and the nasty little gang would set their sights on something else. How wrong could they be?

Poor Losers

A couple of days after the consultant's visit, the grandchildren arrived for a day's entertainment with Grandma and Grandad. They tumbled through the door full of cheerfulness and fun, bringing the house to life. With three small children running about it was not long before the call of nature was felt by one of them.

'Grandma, can you take me to the toilet please?' It was four-year-old Marie, who knew that she was not allowed upstairs on her own. Of course, Grandma dropped what she was doing and took the little girl upstairs to the front bedroom to use the en-suite bathroom. With the child installed on the loo, she stood for a moment, looking out at the lane. As she did so, she was horrified to see, on the opposite side of the road, in Mrs. Lupus's garden, directly in front of the window, an eight-foot effigy of a witch. *My God, these people aren't normal!* She hurried her granddaughter down the stairs as soon as she could, shielding her from the apparition and without a word to Frank. It was so upsetting. What sort of nasty mind conceived that? ... *Joan!*

The witch effigy had been in place for four days when Jenny came to discuss a request from the hospital for Daisy to reconsider her "retirement" from volunteering there. With the kettle coming to the boil, Daisy decided that she ought to tell her friend about the effigy.

'There's something I want your opinion on.' she mentioned, as she poured hot water into the cafetière. Leaving the drinks on the kitchen work surface, she led the way up to the front bedroom. As they entered the room, Jenny gasped in shock at the sight across the road. 'What on earth is that thing in that old woman's garden?' she gasped. 'It *is* her garden isn't it?'

'Mrs. Lupus, It sure is. That's what I wanted your opinion on.'

'I'll tell you my opinion. This cannot carry on!' She said. You have to phone the police. Before his accident, Frank would have stormed over to the neighbour's garden, torn the down the effigy and shoved it in the old hag's face, or worse. He would also have flattened Big Nose long ago, probably both of them!

Daisy knew that her friend's advice was correct and that she could not leave these people to act above the law. She reluctantly picked up the phone and called the local police station. They were both surprised and shocked to be told that an officer would call within the next couple of hours. It would mean that Frank would have to know but he could not be protected from every cruel action; there were so many of them. He listened as the story was related to him and then went slowly upstairs to see for himself. He took the information in with slow nods of his head. It was all being stored away. He never forgot a favour but neither did he ever let a wrong against his family get forgotten. 'I'll leave you to deal with the copper, I'll only forget the facts.' He said, quietly.

Jenny offered to stay until the law arrived, for which, Daisy was grateful and they tried to enjoy the normality of a good old natter while Frank sat down by the river, taking some early summer sun in the garden.

A very efficient looking, female police officer arrived in less than an hour and was shown straight up to the bedroom to see what the problem was. Her shocked reaction was much the same as Jenny's. 'But can you prove who put it up?' Daisy and Jenny sat either side of the constable as all three of them watched the playback from the house camera showing Mrs. Lupus trying first and then the much taller Joan, succeeding in erecting the witch effigy.

'You have a choice: If I go back to the station, I can get some advice and your neighbour will be arrested. Otherwise I can go and see her now and make her remove the effigy straight away. I will put her straight on being neighbourly, while I'm there.'

'Good luck with that!' Jenny snorted.

'I'm really not interested in having her arrested, I'm not interested in her, full stop.' Daisy told her. 'I just want that offensive thing taken down.'

'No worries.' The officer was keen to extend the long arm of the law as far as Mrs. Lupus. She admitted that the first option she had offered, might take days to execute. I'll pop back later and tell you what her excuse is. With that, she left to do her job.

Returning to "Chestnuts" about an hour later, the police officer recounted her visit to Mrs. Lupus: 'She said someone called Gail and Joan had put it up in her garden as a joke because "Old Red lips is putting a shed up". Does that mean anything to you?'

So, Daisy was "Old Red Lips". It followed that they would not like her lipstick: Lupus had never had the first idea of style, even as a young woman, Joan was a singularly ugly, shapeless creature who could easily be either sex. Her shadow, the crooked-nosed Gail, was too immature to know how to apply makeup but too insecure to try it in case Joan disapproved

"Shed" was a reference to the planned extension that they had all opposed and as rude and insulting as ever, just the same as all her "friends" who were all in on the act: Joan, the catalyst to anything unpleasant; the childish Gail; the cake lady who had once seemed a good soul; the lady who talked too much, Mrs. MacDonald, when sober. Most of them joined the wicked old woman whilst she held court, day after day, trying to avoid the dreadful brandy-laced, instant coffee. They were the self-styled "Ladies of Whisperswood". *More like the Bitches of Whisperswood!* It really had become a witch hunt.

The policewoman warned Mrs. Lupus about her behavior, for what it was worth. The local constabulary knew her well. They had been out to her before, she had upset many people by letting her dogs run loose, shouting randomly at people in the street when she had been drinking; after all, she started with brandy-laced coffee at 10 a.m. every day. She was well known locally, as a nasty woman and a bad neighbour. Frank and Daisy could not understand why, in particular, the lady who talked too much should be involved in Lupus's, twisted schemes after the years she had spent as one of her victims. She would tell anyone who would listen, about the dreadful time her family had suffered at the hands of Mrs. Lupus for ten years and now here she was joining her to attack another family. She either had a short memory or was so lonely living with her ancient husband who drank too much. How could anybody be so desperate that they would indulge somebody else was bent on causing misery? It said a lot about her.

    A small success: The witch effigy was taken down.

Chapter Fourteen

The Planning Decision is Made

The day of the planning hearing/appeal was scorching hot, without the merest wisp of cloud in the blue sky and the Bests decided to leave their car in town and walk to the office where the decision would be made. They had no interest in sitting through the case, they were paying an expert to do that for them but knowing the scheduled time for it, they thought it would be nice to hear the verdict as it happened, so to speak.

Arriving at the entrance, to the council offices, they were told by a receptionist that the day's proceedings were just ending and that everyone would be out in about five minutes. She offered them a seat but it was such a hot day that they elected to relax outside on one of the memorial benches dotted about the grounds.

Sure enough, within a few minutes of settling down on a nearby bench, they saw the first of the objectors leaving the building, each with their head down, avoiding eye contact with their intended victims. These were the good people of Whisperswood, no sign of Joan, though; she always operated from behind the scenes.

'Ho-ho! Get a look at this, Daisy!' Frank was belly laughing as he spoke. Mr. Moaning MacDonald was shuffling out through the automatic door, wearing a corduroy jacket, threadbare and patched at the elbows and a long woollen, university scarf, on the hottest day of the year! 'He must have thought it would impress someone!' He gasped through his laughter. 'It's not from the university of life is it?'

The self-important parish councillor really was wearing his old scarf from university days, just so that everyone would know that he had been to one. His round face was red and shiny with sweat. His expression, always glum, was a study in misery: He had lost!   His ancient briefcase, full of important case notes, dangled from one hand. If his humiliation was increased, on hearing the laughter from the bench, it was complete when, right on cue, the one serviceable briefcase catch, pinged open and out fell two pieces of doodle-covered, paper, a child's pencil case and a banana. The latter, thoughtfully packed by Mrs. MacDonald, 'Just in case you feel a little queasy dear.'

Pushing behind MacDonald and in broad contrast to him, came a grinning Mr. Dunn in the company of the chief planning officer who was wearing a broad smile.
'Mr. And Mrs. Best, you have your permission granted.' Said the planner as she shook hands with both of them. 'We can spot a "neighbour gang-up" a mile off. Parish councils don't have any powers, only an opinion but most of them don't understand that, they're all on a power trip.' *Now where have I heard that before?*
Mr. Dunn described how, one by one, the neighbours had stood up and read their objections, none of them valid and all very much, word for word, the same. Finally, Mr. MacDonald had mumbled an introduction for the nobbled local councillor without presenting an objection of his own, at all. The town planners had listened, with increasing impatience, to all the speakers and finally conferred amongst themselves, in whispers, for less than thirty seconds, before simply pronouncing: 'Passed unanimously.'
It was time for a celebratory drink. Frank and Daisy thanked Mr. Dunn for his help and the planning officer for her common sense, before they left to find a bar with outside seating. As they parted company, Frank could not stop himself from giving a wave to the red-faced, nobbled councillor, whose car was refusing to start.

If the Bests thought that they had won their planning permission fair and square and that the gang of bullies would accept defeat, they were wrong. The first bit of fallout came on the Saturday morning following the approval of their planning application.
On Friday evening, Suzy and James called by to see if Frank and Daisy would like to join them for a drink at the village pub. 'Oh. We would love to come with you, but I have a guest checking in to

"Pudding Cottage" later, so I don't think we'll be able to make it.' They had a busy week coming up and socialising would have to take a back seat for a few days.

It so happened that Dan, a mutual good friend, was at The Duke's Head, that evening and seeing them come in, had joined James and Suzy for a drink. They were discussing the planning war over Chestnut Cottage and deciding what they could do to support their victimised friends, when the gang of nasties started to arrive.

Joan's husband, home from the oil rigs, came in with Mr. Big Nose, followed by Mr. "Wandering hands" Jones and Justin, husband of the cake lady who had seemed like a good soul. The man who drank too much arrived, looking suitably lubricated already and finally, making his grand, slow speed entrance, came Moaning Mac. That was the last straw for the couple and with an apology to Dan, they finished their drinks and got up to leave, they could not bear to be within earshot of the curmudgeonly sloth.

Each having bought his own drink, the group of men sat around the only table large enough to accommodate them which was next to the small table occupied by Dan. They invited him to join them and, caught between a rock and a hard place, he politely accepted, stressing that he 'would not be making a night of it.'

The booze began to flow and soon it was taking effect on the less hardened drinkers of the group. The conversation was getting louder and more belligerent, leaving the quiet drinker alarmed to hear that the main subject was how they could take retribution against his friends, the Bests. He heard MacDonald mutter darkly: 'If we're not careful, they're likely to end up with the nicest home in Whisperswood.' "Wandering Hands" Jones was nodding sagely in agreement: 'Except mine of course.'

'Yes, except yours, Jonesy.' Mr. Jones was the only person that Moaning Mac. ever acquiesced to.

Mr. Big Nose, could not hold his drink but, trying to exude testosterone, was doing his best to match Mr. Joan, drinking large single Malts. As he stood up unsteadily, to go to the Gents, he lost his balance and fell across the fat Scotsman, who let out a string of expletives as his whisky spilt all over Jerry Corbinne. Jerry had sidled into the pub alone, after everyone else. He had not contributed anything to the conversation, preferring to just listen, he had been taking advantage of being out alone, to drink lager. He began to snivel with worry that Jane would accuse him of drinking whisky when she smelt it on him. That made Mr. Joan even more angry and he began a rant against all things English.

Dan felt a quiet loyalty to his friends and as the insults against them grew worse, he slowly got to his feet.

'Have another pint…' began "Wandering Hands", drunkenly. Dan wanted to explode with anger but instead, quietly replied: 'Shove it!' Making his position clear. With that, he left for home, thinking that he really ought to let his friends know of the growing hatred for them. The bullies barely glanced in his direction as he left, they were too involved in themselves.

Other locals eating and drinking in the pub, who had been at the sharp end of the same gang before, sat listening in shock. Was there no end to this nasty bunch of idiots, did they never wake up and think about the less fortunate in the world; the poor, the sick or anyone else? Did not one of them realise that we are all here on this earth for a very short period of time and to set out deliberately to hurt and bully and cause untold stress was unbelievable. The "crime" of someone moving into "THEIR" village and daring to want to do their own thing. A man who had suffered a life changing accident wanted to extend his home to make his life simpler. Was that really such a crime?

Coincidental Vandalism?

Frank and Daisy had got wind of the meeting at the pub but couldn't care less. Although life was so busy, they had planned a family day out to the zoo for their little grandson's birthday and they were looking forward to the simple pleasure of it.

That Friday evening, once she got back from "Pudding Cottage", Daisy set to work, preparing a picnic lunch for the next day. Frank was no help in the kitchen, his poor short-term memory and bad eyesight made him more of a liability than a help. It was as if he spent all day saying 'sorry, I didn't see it.' Or 'Sorry, did I just stand on your foot?' as he walked into things and collided with other people. Then there would be a Fall down the stairs, to start the day. She remembered them asking at the hospital how he was coping with life at home. The answer had been that he wasn't! She was having to do everything for him. He had been incapable of finding a tee-shirt in the drawer and a colour-matched pair of socks would be a miracle. They remained optimistic as he, ever so slowly, made tiny steps along the road to recovery.

Everything was prepared for the next day, child seats fitted in the car, the fridge full of food ready to be loaded straight into the cool box. It would be an early start in the morning, not an easy thing for Frank, so an early night was in order.

Daisy was up with the lark in the morning and went straight downstairs to make them both a hot drink. A cup of freshly ground coffee was always a must, to start the day.

When she returned to the bedroom, with the coffee, Frank was in obvious discomfort with his eyes. The sun was already bright in the sky and the forecast was for clear sunshine all day. 'I think I had better stay at home today, It's just going to be too hard for me to walk around in the bright sun, it's not fair on Sam and the little children.' She agreed that what he was suggesting, made sense. There would be enough work to do, looking after the grandchildren, without having to guide her husband through the crowds at the zoo as well.

She decided that she would make it a shorter day than planned. If she left Frank with a lunch prepared, then he would be okay spending the day with his close friend. She rang Jim as she was preparing the lunch and told him the situation. He understood and without hesitation, kept the promise he had made to Daisy as Frank had lain desperately ill in hospital after the accident. He had told her then, to ring him at any time of day or night if they needed help. He was at a loose end all day and would welcome the company of his mate whilst she was away.

'I'll leave a lunch for two, then.' She told him.

'Jim just rang.' She lied to Frank. 'He's coming over to have a look at the bikes, he'll keep you company while I'm gone.' He would be able to enjoy a lay-in for an hour and then ease himself into life. It was relief to her not to have to worry about him.

As she unlocked the back door, she was greeted by the warm air of the glorious morning. The garden was so dry that she had to take the time to go out and water her pots near the back door so they would survive the heat of the day. By the time she was finished, her husband had made his way downstairs for breakfast. She made them each one last coffee and began to pack her bag for the day. She grabbed the picnic from the fridge, along with cold drinks, sweets and nibbles; the children were bound to want a little something to eat during the short journey to the zoo.

With a kiss and a hug for the love of her life, Daisy went out towards the car, walking across the crisp, summer-dry, lawn, to the gravel drive. There were two large ash trees that hung over the drive, that cast a welcome shade across it in the summer, keeping the heat from the car, but Daisy was always careful where she parked as there were pigeons roosting in the trees and boy, oh boy, did they make a mess some days.

As she got nearer to the car, she could see that it was covered in a liquid, splashed over the roof and across the side nearest to the road. She thought: *That doesn't look like pigeon mess.* But she didn't know what it was. The best thing was to put the bags in the car then go and get Frank. When she grabbed the door handle, she discovered that it was also covered in the slimy liquid. She dropped the picnic bag on the front seat of the car and went back to the house to wash her hands and ask Frank to come and see what the problem was.

'What are you doing back here, love, have you forgotten something?' he asked, oblivious to the disaster awaiting him. She instinctively knew that something out of the ordinary was wrong with the car and told him: 'Frank, don't panic and don't run but I need you to come and look at the car, something is wrong.'

'What is it?'

'Well, I don't know. It's covered in some kind of liquid. She returned to the car, with him following behind. Before he even reached the car, Frank called out in alarm: 'Get the hose, quick!'

"Why?' she asked, suddenly worried even more.

'It's paint stripper!' He told her in disbelief. After a life in engineering, he recognised the tell-tale chemical smell, instantly. 'We'll have to phone the police; this has gone too far now!' He said. 'Someone must have thrown it over from outside.'

Daisy unwound the hose and together, they pulled it across the drive to the car. 'How do you know it's paint stripper?'

'Because', he said, 'I know the smell. We used to use it all the time, this stuff's illegal now.'

'Really? I don't think you should wash it off, let's just call the police.' She was very aware that since his accident Frank did not always think things through as he used to.

'No, turn the water on. At least I can try and minimise the damage.' he answered, illogically, as she was getting the phone out of her pocket. He frantically started spraying the car while she rang the police. The police operator informed Daisy that there was an officer literally about to pass near "Chestnuts" and they would divert him to it, to arrive in about five minutes. She relayed the message to Frank, who had finally realised that his efforts with the hose were in vain as the car's paint was damaged too badly for the water to make any difference.

Sure enough, the police car pulled up within about ten minutes of the "101" phone call.

'What are the chances?' Frank said. 'I can't believe that we've called the cops twice and each time they've turned up the same day!' He had a point; we live in a society where ordinarily; a home delivered pizza arrives quicker than the police!

'Thanks for coming so quickly.' Daisy greeted him. 'Bit of a fluke, madam. I've just come on shift and I was on the way to start my patrol. You were just lucky.'

'Not that lucky, I'm afraid.' she replied, pointing at the vandalised car. The constable followed her direction and walked over to the crime scene.

'Looks like some kind of liquid.' He pronounced, looking carefully at the car. 'It is, it's paint stripper.' said Frank , feeling frustrated, from behind him. 'And the paint is bubbling, it has been on a few hours.' The car was in a sorry state.

The policeman looked around at the tall hedge and the solid drive gates. The look on his face was one of confusion. 'Have you been having any problems with anybody recently?' He enquired.

'Well,' Frank began. *Where do I begin?* 'There's a little gang of sore losers here in the village. We have just obtained planning permission to build here and they are beyond livid. They have tried everything they can, to stop us but we were granted permission, with them objecting at every step of the way. They failed and I think this is revenge because we got permission. These aren't normal intelligent people.

'Last night, the same gang of bullies were going to meet at the pub to discuss their next move. And I reckon this was it. My wife came out this morning and found the car like this.'

The police car soon attracted attention. James and Suzy were cycling to work together and pulled up on their bicycles as they drew level with the drive entrance, calling: 'Morning guys. Are you alright? Daisy waved and walked towards them. 'Well, not really.'

'Oh no!' Suzy breathed in a barely audible whisper, followed by: 'What have they done?' as her voice came back. 'What do you mean?' Daisy asked her.

'Well, you know we went to the pub last night, the usual little gang was there, gearing up for trouble. We left when we saw Moaning Mac. come in but Dan was there. You ought to give him a ring and see what went on.' Promising to call in after work, the young couple left her to phone their mutual friend.

Daisy wanted to make sure that the police officer had all the information available while he was there. Once he left, the chances of getting him back would be slim, at best. She rang Dan straight away.

She gave him a very brief account of the situation; the vandalised car, a not very bright copper on the scene and what did he hear at the pub last night? Once he had got over the shock of what had happened, Dan was more than happy to recount what he could remember of the evening's conversation: 'It was the usual crowd.

They started out quiet enough but then the drinking picked up and they got noisier. They were talking about you; they are so mad that you got your planning permission.

'Big Nose was shooting his big gob off as usual, he reckoned he was going to sort you out once and for all. They were all telling him to calm down, he was drinking whisky with Joan's husband; well, he's got Scotch flowing through his veins. Big nose was so drunk, he was all over the place. I told them to cut the nastiness, but they weren't listening, they were all too drunk. I left them to it but I heard Joan's husband say that he would be walking home with Big Nose, he'd probably never have got there on his own.'

She thanked Dan for his help and went back to the police officer, who was laboriously recording contact details from Frank, and told him what Dan had said. The constable pondered this information for a moment then went to inspect the wooden gates for clues, of which there were none that he could see.

The man who would never make detective, stood back and hooked his thumbs in the front of his stab vest. He was about to pronounce on his findings: 'If you think about it,' he said, in his broad Wiltshire burr, 'it would have to be someone tall to have done this.' He turned back to look at the car. 'Also, someone who knew there was a car the other side of the gate, 'cos you can't see it from the road. And it had to be someone with a motive. Have a think who might bear a grudge or have a problem with you.'

To get home from the pub, the inebriated Mr. Joan and Big Nose would have to pass "Chestnuts". And Big Nose was tall. *And I mean, PRETTY tall. Is he crazy as well?* She thought.

The policeman gave them a calling card with a phone number that he assured them would lead to himself. He also assured them that he would 'get to the bottom of this.' and left to 'carry out some enquiries'.

Daisy thought that she had better phone Her son, Sam, who had been expecting her to pick his little family up, over an hour ago. The phone showed four missed calls from him; he would be wondering where they were.

Sam's mobile phone answered before the first ring had finished, he was understandably worried about his mother. 'Sorry, son, I'm running late. I'm just leaving.' She could explain everything when she reached his house. She went back into the cottage kitchen, where Frank was already sitting down after the exertion of the morning. They briefly discussed whether she should cancel the trip to the zoo. 'Absolutely not.' He declared. 'And let that stinking bunch of morons steal a day from us? We'll sort it out later. You go, drive carefully. Give the kids a kiss from me and enjoy the day.'

Jim arrived by motorbike and finding the drive gates open, rode straight in and parked his machine. He let himself into the house with a quick knock on the door as he entered.

'Morning Daisy, I thought you would be long gone by now.' He cheerfully exclaimed in his ignorance. Both she and Frank, tried to put on a brave front but it was difficult. As a good friend, Jim was entitled to an explanation and once Daisy had left for the zoo, his friend gave him a very brief account of the situation, ending with the drama of that morning. Jim listened in shock, to the story, occasionally interjecting with groans, exclamations and snorts.

The grandchildren had a wonderful time at the zoo whilst their parents and grandmother struggled to keep smiling for the sake of the little ones. Daisy just wanted to get back home and be alone with her husband.

It was teatime by the time she did get back. With the best will in the world, there was no way that she could have cut the day short, the grandchildren were enjoying it so much. Frank made no secret of his relief that she had spent the whole day with their son and his children.

The two men had had an enjoyable day together, sitting in the shade, talking men's stuff, once the subject of the local nastiness had been got out of the way. He had initiated the insurance claim for the damaged car, it had to be delivered to the repair shop whenever it was convenient to them. For now, it was time to sit down and discuss the latest challenge.

'The first thing we do is get the CCTV system extended.' It had captured the event of Big Nose having her meltdown in the lane but it did not cover the gates or the driveway. It would have been simple, straightforward evidence of the crime.

'Oh Frank, what a day.' They were both at breaking point but hopefully, the guilty party would be caught and arrested, which would finally send a message to the clique of bullies: 'Stop behaving, like idiots because we will press charges.'

'What do you think?' She said.

'Well, he said thoughtfully, 'if all the "Ladies of Whisperswood" were at Gail's, like Suzy said and their husbands were at the pub, it could very likely have been Big Nose. He's gone past here on his way home, full of booze and thought ah ha! Mr. Joan says: "You ought to give their car a dose of paint stripper, that'll fix 'em." He wouldn't do it himself because he's too much of an old fart, but Big Nose is nice and lanky and young enough, if the old man supplies the paint stripper.'

'Unless it was Joan, on her way home from Gail's in the dark, she is the only other tall person in their gang. After all, the copper said try and think of someone tall. The rest of them are either too feeble or pint sized.' Daisy added. It was a terrible realisation that a jealous neighbour could do such a thing.

They knew that Eric Banks had also been in "The duke's Head" the previous evening and Frank had phoned him earlier that day, to see if he could shed any light on what had happened there. Eric had been cautious with his reply, in fact it was more a case of what he didn't say, but he did confirm that Big Nose was very, very, drunk and shouting in the pub about getting even with the Bests.

Of course, the car was still roadworthy despite the vandalised paintwork, which was now looking worse than ever as the paint stripper continued to eat through to the metal body. Daisy drove it, with Frank to do the talking, to the repair shop, where it was to be surveyed for the insurance claim. The damage was such that there was no doubt that the insurance would pay but ultimately, everybody pays for this type of mindless vandalism. insurance premiums constantly rise with criminal damage. Who does that to someone?

The Insurance Assessor's Story

The insurance assessor, a middle-aged man with the expression of someone who had "seen it all", began his inspection of the damage. As he jotted notes down on a pad, he chatted to them in a friendly manner: So how did this happen?'

'It's a long story that started with a planning issue.'

The assessor stood up and put his pen behind his ear as he looked at his clients. 'Don't tell me,' he said, 'you put in a planning application, the neighbours ganged up, you won, they're mad, so the next morning, Bingo! Your car's trashed!'

'How did you know that?' said Frank.

'Well,' he said, 'I have worked in this body shop for twenty years. Paint stripper and planning applications go hand in hand. Copper got any leads?' It was a pre-requisite of the insurance claim that the police should be involved.

'Not yet.' he replied. Neither did he expect to hear any more from them once they had issued a crime number for the incident.

'No, I've never heard of them finding any guilty parties.', he sympathised. He went on to recount his own extreme experience to them.

'Years ago, I had a planning application in myself. Terrible carry-on; they all wrote their letters of objection, said it would block the light, it would make a mess, make a noise, the list was endless. One particular bloke across the road, caused a lot of trouble, tried get to get everyone to gang up to stop me.

'It was awful for my wife and our baby son. She would leave our cul-de-sac with the babe in a pushchair and not one person spoke to her. It was alright for me, I was at work all day, but she was stuck there with the babe all day, she didn't even feel she could sit in the garden.

'She was becoming anxious, so I put a camera up at the front of the house, just for reassurance. Anyhow, the 6 weeks passed and we got our planning though, we were thrilled, we had never intended to upset anyone. We thought that was it over, we could get on with building our new kitchen. I went out to get in the car for work and guess what? Yep, paint stripper all over it.

Nine out of ten paint stripper jobs we have in here, are related to planning applications. The coppers know that. It brings the green-eyed monsters out. Of course, the wife was upset: "Who's done that to us? it's just awful, I want to move!"

'I told her: "Well we're not moving, they can." When I got home that night, I said to the wife, "I wonder if the camera got the bum that did this." After we'd put the baby to bed, we sat down to look at the tape from the camera. It was just a cheapy, I'd only bought it as a deterrent, but it might have caught something to give us a clue as to what idiot had done it.

'When we finally ran the tape,' He stopped to take a deep breath, the thought of the attack still upset him. Daisy and Frank listened with bated breath. 'And would you believe it? it was the leader of the gang of objectors from across the road. Over he ran, hood up but no doubt it was him, threw the stripper all over the car and ran back into his house. The camera had recorded the lot.

'I rang the coppers; it was hard to get them interested but eventually they came out. The car was written off 'cos the cost of the respray and repair far outweighed its value in the first place. The insurance gave me a car to run around in until it got sorted. A couple of days later, the copper came back to see us. "Do you want to press charges?"

'"I sure do." I told him.

'"Well, if you take this step, it is a serious one..."

'"Bring it on." I told him. So, it went to court, the bloke was found guilty, fined £2000 plus costs and given two months in prison. The court ordered him to move to a new address and his house was put on the market by the courts and he had to accept any offer that the court deemed reasonable, and he couldn't live within a two-mile radius of us. He's been gone years, we built our kitchen, the wife's happy, so am I. You know what they say: "Happy wife, happy life."

'So, you make sure, when you get the slime ball, make sure they take him to court and make sure you win. They're scum bags. But you know, the stuck-up bunch are the worst kind but they always make a mistake, usually bragging about it. You know what they say: "Loose lips sink ships."' The assessor liked his little quotes.

'It might take a while but you'll get him, he'll always be looking over his shoulder.'

Having finished his story and offered his well-meant advice, the man completed his survey of the car and assured them that he would contact them the next day with a date to commence the repairs. He was very sympathetic and it was some small comfort to discover that theirs was not a unique case.

True to his word, the assessor phoned the next afternoon with a date for them to leave the car with his company. He expected it to take another few weeks at least, before it would be returned to "better than new" condition at the expense of the insurance company. The repair bill was just under £12,000, which would have made it a write off had it not been such a low mileage vehicle. That was a shocking amount of damage.

Mr. And Mrs. Banks's Dilemma

By the time the day came for the car to be delivered to the repair shop, there was so much talk in the village that the Bests could "feel" the whispers as they went about their day. The rumour mill had been working overtime; everyone knew about the vandalism of the car and was horrified that it had happened. All except one person.

Everyone had a theory but only a select few actually knew who the culprit was and they were not saying. To stay in the clique was the most important thing; the pecking order was strict, with Joan as the head honcho. Everyone else in it had to toe the line.

That evening, Bunny and Eric came over to "Chestnuts" to offer their friends some moral support. Daisy opened the door. 'Hi Eric, come on in. Bunny followed with a bunch of flowers for the house. They all sat down in the gazebo by the river. 'Drink anyone?' *Of course, they do.* Daisy thought to herself with a smile.

'Oh yes, Eric said, 'just a quick one as you're offering.' She went back into the house with Bunny to fill the drinks order. Whisky was always Eric's favourite tipple while the rest of them would enjoy a chilled glass of Chablis. The ladies brought the drinks out to the gazebo along with some cheese and crackers to accompany the wine, a spare bottle of which, Bunny was carrying in a terracotta cooler.

They drank a toast to happy days, after which, Daisy came straight to the point over something that had been on her mind all day. 'Eric, do you know who did that to our car?'

'No!' said Eric, he was a bit startled at the forthright question and appeared taken off guard. Bunny glanced at her husband in a way that said, "If you do know, you had better say!" Composing herself again, she asked for a top up of Chablis.

It was a difficult situation for Eric and Bunny. If they had heard who the culprit was and they coughed, they would have no friends in the village, tricky when you are leaving a holiday home empty for months on end. Bunny had downed her wine and followed it with a couple of generously poured G&Ts, if not enough gin to sink a battleship, then a small gunboat. 'Well,' she said, 'it's got to be the gang, but which one, is anybody's guess. All they ever do is talk about you.' It was Eric's turn to shoot her a warning glance now.

Ignoring his warning, she continued, 'Moaning Mac is always asking Eric about you, he told them straight, didn't you, Eric.

'I told them I am not an information service. It was him and "Wandering Hands" Jones. "What do you know about them up at "Chestnuts"?" I said to them, "If you want to know about them, knock on the door" ... They haven't been, have they?'

Bunny cut in, 'Mary Mac told me she knows who did it but she wouldn't say, she said Joan had phoned Moaning Mac. and told him. They are so jealous of you both, that's all they talk about.'

'Well hopefully,' said Frank, 'the police will speak to them all and sort this out.'

'The police are useless.' Eric snorted. 'They won't do anything to these people round here, they think they are so grand with their swanky fat wallets, the police are frightened of them because they start banging out their fancy letters from their expensive lawyers. Plod will go around giving lip service and do nothing. Now be a pal won't you and top this glass up.'

The days dragged on. They had the feeling that the police knew who the perpetrator was but could take no action without proof or evidence…. or the will to do anything. Eventually the car was returned to them, resplendent with a completely new paint job. The policeman did get back with an update: He had conducted 'extensive enquiries' and even asked the number one suspect, face to face, if he was responsible for the vandalism. The number one suspect had denied it (surprisingly!) and that had put an end to the constable's 'extensive enquiries', the case was officially closed.

Chapter fifteen

Building gets underway

The thunderous rattle of a caterpillar tracked digger reversing precariously off the back of a low loader, shattered the early morning tranquility of Whisperswood. It heralded the arrival of Tom Crapper, the ground worker, out in the lane outside "Chestnuts". It was seven o'clock in the morning! He came highly recommended by one of Frank's contacts in the building trade and as he jumped, grinning, from the digger's cab, he was already on his mobile phone, organising the other trades who would be helping him.

Tom set to work as soon as his machine was in place and worked steadily for two hours when he stopped for his first cup of tea, surrounded by what looked like random piles of earth and rock. He had transformed part of the garden into a moonscape, but he knew what he was doing.

From the kitchen, Daisy gave a satisfied smile as she heard the excavator start up after just ten minutes of inactivity, only for it to stop almost immediately. She could hear Tom shouting in the distance. *What on earth is he doing?* Her first thought was that he must have damaged something with the business end of his machine.

Tom was now knocking politely on the back door. For such a big man, working as he did, in a rough, tough environment, his knock was surprisingly dainty. She opened the door to find the workman standing, caked in mud to his knees, with a puzzled look on his face. 'There's some woman filming me through the hedge!'

'What do you mean, "filming" you?' It was her turn to look puzzled.

'Some woman.' He repeated. 'she's got a hell of a Conk on 'er.'... *Big Nose!*

Daisy saw red. The prying Gail just could not help herself! Slipping on a pair of gardening shoes, she rushed outside, past Tom and made straight for the open drive gates. As she reached the road outside, Gail jumped like a startled hare and made off in the opposite direction, trying to stuff a smart phone into her pocket. Daisy was too shocked to challenge her and decided to ignore it. She told Tom to carry on but to let her know if anymore "investigators" turned up.

The industrious ground worker put in long working days while a small fleet of lorries removed the spoil he created and delivered ready-mixed concrete which he expertly disposed of in all the right places. He would soon be ready for Darren and his men to take over.
Every day, Joan came trudging by with her dogs, straining to see what was happening in the garden of "Chestnuts". In the afternoons she took to parking her rusty old estate car, easily recognisable by the registration: JAB123, close by, while she ran some imaginary errand. Frank joked that it stood for: 'Joan's A Bitch'.
Both Mary and Moaning Mac. Suddenly found a need to drive their respective cars up as far as the cottage to turn around every day, in order to drive back and park outside their own house. It was always easy to tell when Moaning was manoeuvring his car outside, because he drove as painfully slowly as he did everything else. Mary had taken the plunge and bought her own car many years before, when she still had a say in her own life, because her husband had declared that her driving was too dangerous for her to be allowed behind the wheel of his car.
The man who drank too much, had invested in a new pair of binoculars but even he found the need to walk his diminutive dog past the front of Chestnut Cottage as Tom was leaving work one afternoon. It was however, a one-off; to such a tiny dog, the expedition must have been exhausting, never to be repeated.
Only Mrs. Rose was direct enough to ask Mr. Crapper what exactly he was doing as she had a copy of the plans but, not being very skilled in that field, she did not know how to read them. Calling through the same hole that Gail had used to get her photos, part of the damage that Mrs. Rose herself, had wrought on the hedge

eighteen months earlier, she had caught the digger driver off guard while he was measuring a trench. She was sure that the shapes he had made were not the same as the ones on the drawings she had got from the council. Mr. Crapper very patiently listened to her then kindly told her: 'Oh dear, my love, I don't know about things like that.' With a smile, he had touched the peak of his "JCB" baseball cap and climbed back into his cab. As he pushed the starter button, Mrs. Rose had been enveloped in a cloud of black diesel exhaust and wisely withdrew to the safety of her garden, none the wiser for her effort.

A Little Light Relief

    Tom Crapper had very skillfully kept the disruption of the garden to a minimum however, any untouched areas of grass were now piled high with building materials. On this lovely summer evening, there were limited options for sitting in the garden, enjoying the view. It was a good enough reason to go out for a pleasant evening drink whilst relaxing outside "The Dukes Head".
    Instead of going directly to the pub, Frank and Daisy left the road and took to the fields, following narrow rights of way to get a little exercise. It was a pleasant roundabout route to "The Duke's Head" that they had taken many times. On most days, it was a popular area for day trippers and walkers but by the evening, they were all long gone, back to their own towns and villages. At this time of day, the long grass either side of the narrow track was alive with the buzzing of summer insects and the trees and shrubs, populated by little birds, singing, the only sound to break the silence.
    The couple hadn't gone very far before they heard voices on another track that ran parallel to theirs, behind dense bushes which hid them from view. As they drew level to the voices, they recognised them as belonging to Jane and Jerry Corbinne. Jane was cursing: 'For Christ sake, Jerry, there is dog poo on my shoe! That bloody woman, Joan and her dogs! She walks them here every day and this

is where they relieve themselves. She never picks it up and there she is at the parish council, complaining "there's no dog poo fairy".' She did a fair impersonation of the other woman. 'And it's her dogs that make all the mess in the village! Oh, for goodness sake, Jerry you haven't got it all, I can still smell it.'

'Well, rub your foot on the grass, Jane.', Reasoning.

'Don't tell me what to do.' Angrily.

'Well it was you that stood in it.' Meekly.

'Yes and if her dog hadn't done it, it wouldn't have happened. Jerry, when we get home, you need to write a letter to the parish council about all the dog mess in this village. Make it anonymous and put in the letter that you have seen Joan's dogs do it.

'Every single time we go for a walk we are dodging dog shit. You write that letter, Jerry, the minute we get in. If you care about me, you'll do it. Do you hear me?'

'I will I will.' he said in an effort to placate her.

The eavesdroppers were doubling up with silent laughter, at the entertainment of "Yah yah" losing her temper. Gone were the airs and graces.

Suddenly they heard Jerry stammering: 'Oh, H-Hello J-Joan. Fancy seeing you here.'

'My bloody husband came home today so I am out! With my doggies of course.' She sounded pretty drunk, which was the norm for her on any evening.

'What's she doing out at this time of day? I'm surprised she can still stand up!' Frank whispered between giggles.

Jane had quickly recovered her composure and was greeting the old gossip as if she was a long-lost friend. They could hear the couple petting and cooing over Joan's dogs.

The smell of fresh dog toilet came wafting through the bushes and it was time to quietly move on without letting the laughter out. They left the hapless trio, who all disliked each other, to their shallow small talk.

Sitting outside "The Duke's Head", twenty minutes later, the story of the Corbinnes and the dog mess was entertaining the other drinkers as our heroes refreshed themselves.

Cracking On

Once Daryll arrived on site, the drone of the digger was replaced by the cheerful banter of his little team of men and the music from his ever-present radio. No matter what they were doing, the radio always had to be set up first, it was, without doubt, the most important piece of equipment in his van. As long as it was on, they worked harder and faster than any team of builders in the Cotswolds.

Each day, as he was finishing work, Daryl gave Daisy a list of things he would need for the next couple of days and she would make sure it was delivered in time. It suited both the builder and his customer as it relieved him of a lot of tedious paperwork and running around, while at the same time, she kept a close eye on the budget and knew that everything would keep running smoothly. There were no wasted man hours, waiting for supplies and the workmen were always busy. Frank was guiding her over the technical issues but she was managing the project with maximum efficiency.

The garage was completed, and Daryl had detailed his men to move its inventory of engineering equipment and tools into it, ready for action. Frank was in his element. They had never owned a house without a garage before and now things were becoming more normal.

'I've left space at this end to stack all the stuff we need to keep dry when we start the extension, you've got bags of room left for all that old bike stuff you like.' He was standing on the scaffold that the roofers had recently vacated and laughing as he spoke, but it made sense to have a dry storage area for anything fragile. 'Looks like you've got a visitor.' He added from his vantage point.

It was another good friend, from the other end of the village.

'Hi Frank, I thought I should let you know, that little crowd of parish council troublemakers had another one of their meetings at the pub, last night. I'm afraid that your place was on the agenda again. They are trying to find a way to sabotage your building and stop it going ahead.' He had no time to stop but simply wanted to help a friend in need. Frank thanked him and thought no more about the warning. He could not think of anything else unpleasant that could happen, the garage was finished, with no problems and the rest of the works were ahead of schedule. Besides, there was too much to concentrate on with Daryl's team of men starting work the next day, on the actual house extension. Tom Crapper had left everything ready for them to begin and the builder was itching to get started.

The Enforcement Officer

The scaffolders who had surrounded the embryonic garage with their spider's web of tubes and boards were now back, to take it all down again and reveal the finished building. The drive gates were open, with their lorry parked across the driveway so there was nothing to stop the latest unexpected visitor from walking straight into the property.

'Morning. I'm looking for Mister or Mrs. Best.' he called to Daryl, who was busy supervising the scaffold team. The man had a lanyard with some kind of identity card around his neck and was holding a clipboard. In Daryl's opinion, he did not look as if he had been invited by either Mister or Mrs. Best.

'Better knock on the door, mate!' He called back, not leaving his position, halfway up the partially dismantled scaffolding. He had no time for people with clipboards, they usually meant trouble. In this case he was right.

'Well, I suggest you stop what you are doing right now, this is an illegal development.' A very authoritative voice.

Daryl ignored him. 'Don't put that b……. scaffold board there, mate, it'll fall on the radio!' He shouted at a brawny scaffolder who was sweating under the weight of two long planks of wood. Daryl was very fussy about his radio, it had to be just right for his brick layer.

The clipboard-carrying visitor picked his way to the back door of the cottage and knocked sharply. His blood pressure was rising, the rude builder had annoyed him to the point where, come what may, he would have that man's work pulled down…. by law!

Frank answered the knock on the door, his wife standing at his shoulder. The visitor introduced himself.

'My name is Mr. Hurt... as in John. I am the enforcement officer from the council planning department.' He announced, holding his ID up for effect. *So that's what they were up to!*

Frank knew exactly what the man meant but he said, 'What do you mean, John?' With a bemused expression.

'As in John Hurt, the actor.' Mr. Hurt explained, struggling to retain his official composure.

'Oh.' Replied Frank, with a faraway look on his face. 'Why not say: "As in Locker"? You know, the film, "The Hurt Locker." He could feel his wife, poking him in his back and sense her shaking with silent giggles.

Mr. Hurt's face was turning scarlet from the neck up. He was going to explode at any second and some rapid de-fusing was called for.

Daisy interrupted her husband's baiting of the unwelcome visitor with: 'How can we help you Mr. Hurt?' As if nothing had been said by Frank.

'I have received a complaint that you have demolished a stone wall that has a preservation order on it and are making a new access onto the highway without planning permission.'

'Really?' She said, puzzled. 'We're not doing anything of the sort.'

Mr. Hurt's face was returning to a more normal colour and he controlled his earlier anger to the point where he was able to converse with Mrs. Best in a reasonable manner.

'Well, I can see a pile of stone that looks as if it used to be a wall and you have a large area of dead hedge which looks as if it is going to be a new opening from your property. It's probably just envious neighbours.' he advised her. 'It usually is; they see a nice extension going up and think it isn't fair, so they call my department. Most of my visits are a waste of time, but you understand, I do have to pay a visit and take a look.

'Of course.' She agreed. 'You had better show me where you mean.' She picked up a copy of the planning application and permission from a little table by the door as she left to follow him to the scene of the crime. Daryll had advised them to keep it there in case of just such an eventuality.

Together, they walked around the piles of scaffold and the empty coffee mugs, to the demolished wall. The man from the council pointed at it and declared: 'That wall had a preservation order on it, you cannot do anything to it, it will have to be rebuilt and the design of your extension will have to be altered and re-submitted for planning approval. I advise you to stop all work now or I shall have to call the Police. You might as well send your builders home.'

Daisy calmly shuffled through her papers. 'Let me show you the map....'

'I have seen the map, madam.' He cut in abruptly, 'and that wall should not have been demolished without permission.'

'Then I suggest you look at it again.' She replied, opening up the surveyor's drawing for him to see. Pointing at the protected wall in the drawing, she said to him, 'Do you mean this one here?'

'That's the one. You see? Protected!' He answered triumphantly.

Daisy pointed to an old stone wall running along the edge of the garden with the enforcer's gaze following. She could see his face reddening again as he realised his mistake.

'That's your "protected wall", Mr. Hurt. This was an old goat pen or something that we knocked down. All the permissions are there in black and white. Believe me, with the sort of people that live around here, we wouldn't try anything that wasn't sanctioned by the council.'

The enforcement officer realised his obvious mistake as soon as he saw the wall that she was pointing at. He had taken the anonymous complainant at their word and not done his homework properly. Now he had to extricate himself from the embarrassing situation. He consulted his clipboard.

'Okay, I can strike that off.' He said as if he was doing them a favour. 'I just need to deal with the access onto the road that you are creating.'

'We spent eight thousand pounds on automatic gates, we're not likely to make another entrance next to them but you had better show me what you mean.'

Mr. Hurt led her back through the garden and out through the open gates, onto the road outside and began walking along towards the red brick cottage belonging to the Rose Family.

Daisy had not been along here for quite some time as controlling the tradesmen had kept her busy enough and gardening had been on the back burner.

As they drew opposite the red brick cottage, she saw with a gasp of horror, what the enforcement officer was talking about. She poked at the hedge that she had been painstakingly nurturing back to health after its near destruction, by Mrs. Rose.

Sure enough, about a ten-foot length of holly hedge was visibly dead or dying. The enforcement officer held his arm out horizontally in front of the dead hedge to emphasise the complaint.

'This is what I'm here about.' He said apologetically.

'Oh No!' Daisy's reaction was disbelief. 'Someone's poisoned my hedge!' She groaned. 'I have been trying to recover this poor hedge ever since we moved in.' She explained to the now sympathetic, Mr. Hurt, who was not really sure what he could say to comfort her.

'Well I can see that the only illegal activity going on here is the attack on your hedge. I am very sorry to have troubled you, Mrs. Best. I shall write up my report when I get back to the office but I have to warn you, It looks like you have a neighbour somewhere who won't take "no" for an answer. I hate to say it but I fear I may be back again but rest assured, I will attach the correct priority to any further complaints I get regarding your building works.'

He went to get into his car but stopped and turned to face her again. 'Err, I was a little abrupt with your builder when I first arrived, do you think you could pass on my apology to him please?'

'Of course. Don't worry.' The tables had turned in quite a productive manner. They now had the town's enforcement officer on their side.

As she walked back to the house, Daryl was filling in the Scaffold boss about the creepy neighbours that he may well encounter.

'I'm sorry about that, Daryl. He made a mistake; you can keep working.'

'Don't worry about it, Lady Bee. It happens all the time in places like this. I didn't stop anyway; I'm used to it.' he replied with a laugh. 'I turned the radio off though, so we could hear what was going on! We haven't been able to do much without any music!' Turning towards his labourer, he called, 'You can put it back on now, Chaz!'

The dying hedge was a puzzle but Daisy thought back to the conversation that Frank had had with Pod Rose when he had first met that family. There was the bit about how their sitting room "used to be pitch black before but not anymore." At the time, they had not been able to work out what he had meant by that. Now it was clear: No, it wasn't going to be dark in his house anymore because he had put weed killer on the hedge and killed it! *What's going to happen next?* Mr. Rose just had not realised how long it would take for the hedge to die, having poisoned it the day Chestnut cottage went up for sale.

Daryl was a real family man and had booked to take his little brood on holiday, long before the planning permission for Chestnut Cottage had been granted but he promised Frank that the garage would be completed and fitted out before he left on his vacation. He was as good as his word, with one day to spare, which left the Bests with ten days on their own to tidy up, before the builder returned from Disney World.

Life at "Chestnuts" was pleasantly quiet, without the daily routine of tradesmen and deliveries from the builder's merchant. Daisy managed to save a few shrubs that had suffered collateral damage from the workmen and mowed the grass where the piles of building supplies had been. Every evening that Daryl and his men had been there, she had religiously cleared up the detritus left by them and had eventually filled a skip with building waste. The skip could finally go and now they were ready to start all over again with the house extension.

Life changes

Having already given up her voluntary work at the hospital, Daisy made the decision to stop the prison visiting as well. She needed to spend more time at home, helping her husband and enjoying their grandchildren.

With her usual box of bits and pieces sitting beside her on the passenger seat, she set off on the forty-five-minute drive to the prison. On arrival, the box of bits and pieces was taken from her and checked while she went through the familiar security checks. Over the years, she had got to know the prison staff quite well and they were all sorry to hear that it was to be her last visit.

She settled herself into the small prison library where the literacy help was on offer each Friday and waited for her little group of young offenders to be let in. She emptied the box of its contents which comprised a variety of cards, greetings, congratulations, plain notelets, as well as a collection of postcards. The idea was that the lads would be encouraged and able to write to their families; their children, sweethearts, Mums and Dads, when they no longer had her to help.

It was a great feeling for Daisy that she had helped these young prisoners to maintain contact with the outside world by helping them to read and write. A couple of them in particular, had earned her sympathy; they had both had really a tough start but had made such good progress that she had high hopes of them leading meaningful lives in the future. Without literacy, rehabilitation outside would be far harder for her students but her feelings were about to be jolted.

The informal education and help session was drawing to an end and the lads were divvying up the writing things that she had brought. There was a general embarrassed shuffling among the young men and a couple of them were pushed to the fore, one of them, holding something behind his back.

'We're really sorry you're leaving Mrs. Best, you've been great. We've done a card for you.' he said, blushing from head to toe. He drew his hand from behind his back and handed her a large homemade card signed by each of them. On the front they had written: "Thanks for everything We will miss you". There was a surprisingly detailed drawing, in ball point pen, of a bunch of flowers. Inside, each of the eight lads had written a message and signed the card. At the beginning of the "course", none of them had been able to write more than his name and that, poorly. This was one of the most touching moments of her life.

When she left, three hours later, she was also carrying a bouquet of flowers, given to her by the appreciative prison officers, who had had a whip-round. With a heavy heart, Daisy put the flowers and the card, which she would treasure, on the back seat of the car and started the journey home.

She had just turned into Whisperswood when she had to slow to a crawl in order to avoid running over the lady who talked too much and her husband, who drank too much, as they staggered, arm in arm, down the middle of the road. The lady who talked too much, heard the car and turned around, to look. In the process, she fell into her husband and the pair of them collapsed in a heap, rolling up against the verge, snorting with alternate drunken curses and drunken.

'Sorry, Daisy. Liquid lunch. Whoops!' gurgled the lady who talked too much, as Daisy drove round and past them. They must have been to yet another drinking session in the village, this time disguised as lunch.

The drive gates at home were open and she recognised the council enforcement officer's car parked in the drive along with another, which she also knew but could not think who it belonged to. Her immediate concern was for Frank, he would not know where the paperwork was to fend off this visit.

'Thank goodness you're home, darling. That chap turned up again.' He said, giving her a kiss on the cheek.

'Yes, I recognised his car. Who's with him in the other one?'

'Don't worry, it's Anna's.'

When the man from the council knocked, Frank had made him wait while he got some help. He had phoned Daisy's niece, Anna, who ironically, was a senior planning officer for the County Council. She had left work and hurried round, taken the paperwork from her uncle and then taken charge of the situation. Mr. Hurt would have his work cut out if he had to argue with Anna!

Daisy went straight out to find them, measuring distances and angles. Mr. Hurt greeted her with the news that he had received a complaint that the garage had been built larger than agreed and too close to the property boundary.

'It certainly has not!' Daisy fumed.

'Well, as I told you last time: unfortunately, I have to investigate every complaint. I know you have a few difficult people in this area, we get to know who is genuine and who is just malicious'

Anna was well and truly, on the case and told her Aunt to leave her to deal with the enforcement officer as they both spoke the same language. Apart from which, she had him eating out of her hand.

With everything that could be measured, measured and everything declared within limits, Mr. Hurt was once again apologising for his intrusion. He and Anna were getting on like old friends and he was giving her the lowdown on some of his visits to the village.

'I come here more often than any other village in my area; nearly always malicious. Ironically, the three genuine calls I've had, have all been about people on the parish council who think they're above the law. In every case, they had to do remedial work.'

It turned out that Mrs. Rose had made a complaint about the cake lady's husband, who had slowly and quietly been extending his house, which was listed, and as such, could not be altered. As a result, the cake people had been ordered to demolish everything that they had added. She had quite rightly said that she had to obey the rules, so why shouldn't they? She obviously did not think that obeying the rules, extended to other people's hedges though.

'And don't get me started on the MacDonalds. He's been adding bits on, trying to sell junk from his house, forever. The guy's a clown and he's sitting in judgement of others.'

As they walked to their cars, he assured Anna that he would contact her via her direct line at the County Council should any more issues arise, concerning her Aunt's property.

There was nothing left for them to talk about and Anna's body language was sending the message that he should get in his car and leave. After a moment's hesitation, he plucked up the courage (nothing ventured, nothing gained!) to mention to her, that should there ever be a vacancy at "County", he would be very keen to attend the interview for it.

'well, I'm sure if a position arises, you will hear of it via internal memo.' She brushed him off.

Anna relayed the good news to her Aunt and Uncle that there was no problem with the building and she told them what Mr. Hurt had said about the parish councillors, which gave everyone a good laugh. They were so grateful for Anna's help but she told them that, as she was technically, Mr. Hurt's superior, there was never any doubt that the problem would go away and she had rather enjoyed getting away from the office for a bit.

Her husband was also a planning officer in another jurisdiction and had written many guides on planning laws, he was a well-known and respected author on the subject.

He always said that if you wish to complain about a neighbour's planning application, be very careful, as you will have to live with that decision. It rarely ends well. Nearly all objections are based on jealousy; if I haven't got it, you can't have it either.

Another of his quotes was from an oncologist friend. He had treated two cases of breast cancer in the last six months that were both directly linked to stress caused by nasty neighbours ganging up and objecting to planning applications.

'It's still Friday, let's go out and have a little celebration. Fancy eating out at "Parsley House?"

'why not? Bunny and Eric are over here on holiday, I'll see if they want to join us?'

"Parsley House" was their favourite restaurant at the moment; a small bistro in the next town. The venue was a well-kept secret, that served Michelin quality food, created by a top flight chef, who liked to keep a select small clientele. Frank and Daisy knew him from years before when he had been working for an agency at pubs and he had never forgotten their generosity to him when he was struggling. There was always a table for them at his Bistro.

Daisy volunteered to drive, so that her husband could enjoy a drink with Eric and Bunny, who they stopped to pick up on the way.

'We've never heard of "Parsley House", Bunny said, as the pulled away from their cottage. 'Eric asked Moaning Mac and he said it's only a bistro, not even a restaurant and we won't get much choice there.'

'That's how much he knows. I doubt he can afford to go there, actually.' Frank retorted. 'Trust me, Eric, you will enjoy this experience.'

Following the entry road into town, they needed to turn left by a kebab van, standing under a tall floodlight on some waste ground. The entrance to the small "Parsley House" car park was directly opposite the kebab van's pitch. Driving in, Daisy parked up in the last remaining space and they all got out, chatting. She looked around and it was impossible to miss, under the glare of the floodlight: none other than Moaning Mac. Pushing a Donner kebab into his mouth with both hands. She called the others' attention to the ironic sight.

'Look over there everybody, it's moaning Mac. The man who won't eat at "Parsley House" because it's just a bistro.' The parish councillor heard their laughter and looked in their direction but, floodlit as he was, he could not see who was in the gloom of the carpark. Then, 'Hello, Mac!' Eric shouted across the tarmac, giving his identity away. The self-proclaimed gastronome put two and two together, remembering that Bunny and Eric were dining at the "Parsley House" that night. Horrified, he glanced at the floodlight then back at the brightly lit kebab van and realised his predicament. They were all looking at him, caught red handed in his natural eating habitat; with chili sauce, spilt down the front of his holed pullover. He abruptly turned through one hundred and eighty degrees to face the van and hide his features from them but it was too late, his secret was out.

The pompous kebab scoffer pretended not to hear. Instead, he attempted, desperately, to engage the kebab seller in animated conversation for the benefit of his audience, who could not stop laughing. He could make out several different voices in the carpark: It had to be the bests there with the Bankses. The blank expression on the face of the kebab vendor, showed that he spoke only enough English to sell his wares; he could not understand and had no interest in, the scruffy old man, talking gibberish at him.

Eric grumbled: 'To hear him speak, you'd think he only dined on the finest food and wore silk everything. Look at him, Kebab in his fat gob and a phony education up his backside!'

'Oh, forget it, Eric.' Daisy gently chided him. We've had a laugh; he's got to live with himself.'

When they entered the bistro, Bunny and Eric were immediately impressed by the lovely rustic ambiance that Daisy had already described to them. A convenient table for four was reserved for them in a discreet corner of the busy eatery. Needless to say, the meal was everything they expected and more. Finally, after exquisitely homemade after- dinner mints and the best arabica coffee, it was time to leave.

'I think you must be right; that moaning old fool has never been here, we'll definitely come here again.' Eric enthused, as they said their goodnights to the bistro's owner/chef and his staff.

Chapter seventeen

Jane and The Scaffolders

Daryl had made great progress on the new extension to Chestnut Cottage. He had reached as far as he could go from the first lift of scaffold and was waiting for the scaffold company to arrive to fit the next level, which would enable him to get started, building the roof.

'Lady Bee, you need to move your car; the scaffolders are on their way. If they can get their wagon right in, it'll be quicker getting the job done.'

Daisy moved her car out of the drive and parked it a little way down the lane. As she locked it, she caught sight of Jane Corbinne peering out of her front room window at her. The window was so dirty besides being mostly obscured by overgrown weeds and shrubs that it seemed hardly worth while trying to see through it.

The scaffolders arrived just as Daisy walked back into the driveway. With no time to lose, the men jumped down from the cab, each one shouting, 'Hello, Lady Bee!' as they reached the ground and began unloading their gear. The "Lady Bee". Moniker had been learnt from Daryl and was an affectionate joke, they all loved Daisy for her generous friendliness.

They were a tough bunch of men to look at but every one of them was a hardworking, gentle diamond. These men would gladly help anyone who needed a hand, they always went the extra mile and tried their best to keep the customer happy through such a stressful time as having a home clad in metal pipework.

Her reply to the greetings was, 'I suppose you all could do with a cuppa.' To which she received a chorus of different requests: 'Two sugars please';

'No milk for me' thanks';
'Can I have a coffee, four sugars please?'

She assured them that it would be coming up, all the while trying to remember the different orders. She was in the kitchen manning the kettle, so missed Jane's not so, dramatic arrival.

Standing on the road, next to the back of the scaffold lorry, which was sticking a couple of feet out of the drive entrance, She craned her chubby neck left and right, repeatedly calling: 'excuse me', her voice lost in the racket of rattling scaffold tubes and clamps as they were dumped unceremoniously from the lorry onto the ground.

Eventually, Steve, the gaffer, spotted her, by now, waving frantically at him. He had no idea who she was but thought she must need help with something. She did, in a way.

'Hello love, you alright? I wouldn't stand there too long; you might get whacked by a lump of something.'

'What on earth are you doing?' Jane pulled a face showing her disgust at the coarse way in which this scruffy man spoke to her.

Steve turned to look at his scaffold lorry theatrically, looked back at his interrogator and said, 'Putting up a bit of scaffold, love. Do you need some doing as well?'

'Of course not!', she angrily retorted. 'You're making an awful lot of noise here. I work hard and today is my day off, I would like a little peace and quiet, thank you very much! I don't think you have permission to put that, that, stuff up.' she said, pointing at the short length of scaffold tube he was holding.

'I see.' He said with mock understanding. 'Well my first observation is that you're a bit nosy. Secondly, you're getting on my nerves now, I'm a busy bloke, I don't need to be wasting time here. Best you tell someone who's interested in what you've got to say.' He turned to carry on working.

'I've got the phone number off your lorry.' she retorted. 'You'll have no job tomorrow; I'm going to ring your boss!'

'Okay, but you'll be talking to me, so don't do it just yet, I'm busy at the moment.' he told her, as he walked away. He briefly looked over his shoulder at her and added, just to make it clear to her, 'I am the boss, it's my firm.' He did not miss Jerry, hiding down the road, calling to his wife as loudly but quietly as he could, 'come back, Sweetest.'

As his men put the finishing touches to the scaffolding, Steve told Daisy about the "snooty neighbour".

'Oh no! I'm sorry about that, Steve, I saw her hovering about when I moved the car. I should have known she was out for trouble.'

'Don't worry about it, love. I bet, for fifty per cent of our jobs, we turn up and the neighbour starts kicking off. It's a pain in the backside but it's just part of the job. Then in six months' time, they are having work done themselves and want scaffolding of their own put up. That's when I think to myself, "hang on, aren't you the one that was complaining when I was last in this area?" and so it goes on.'

The bustle of activity at the entrance to "Chestnuts' attracted Mary Mac. Who just happened to need a walk as far as the cottage, where she slowly turned round, her eyes roaming over the new building work and then disappeared whence she had come, frantically scribbling notes in a well-thumbed reporter's note book. Mrs. MacDonald missed nothing.

Italy

The building project was going so well, that Frank and Daisy relented when their daughter suggested that they took a break from the 'coalface' and go away for a week's holiday with their friends in Italy. It was arranged that their son, Sam would move into the cottage as standby project manager just in case Daryl came up against anything unexpected. Both "Christmas" and "Pudding" Cottages were fully booked so Louise could easily keep an eye on them. What could go wrong?

There was just the matter of listing all the instructions for Sam, covering every eventuality. They were forgetting that their offspring had grown up surrounded by building works and property development plans.

Daisy booked last minute flights from Gatwick while Frank rang their friends in Verona to warn them of the impending visit. Gino and his wife, Lucia, were overjoyed at the news and naturally insisted that they stay with them as their guests, while they were in Italy. They were already planning a full program of entertainment and meetings with old acquaintances.

The next day, the Bests were off to relax in the sun for a few days.

The two couples had been firm friends for thirty years after the men had worked together in Germany all that time ago. Most summers, the two couples took turns to host each other in their own country but this was a welcome surprise to them all. Lucia alerted all the neighbours who arranged to come over to their vineyard for a slap-up meal to welcome the guests.

Warm continental, evenings were spent sitting out on the terrace chatting in English and Italian, over salads fresh from Gino's garden, followed by pasta dishes which in turn were followed by wonderful desserts brought along by different neighbours each day. This was real community living, with never a crossed word or snide comment from anybody.

They sailed on Lake Garda, Visited More friends in the Dolomites, where they sailed more small boats, ate local food in tiny "trattorias" and generally lived la vita bella for a few days. Whisperswood and its problems were a world away and was forgotten to the point that they did not bother about checking in with Sam or Daryl. What could go wrong anyway?

On the last night, the four friends went to the famous Verona Arena and watched Verdi's "Aida". It was strange to think that their first visit to the opera here, with Gino and Lucia, had been as young, thirty somethings. Some friendships go on forever.

It was another whirlwind week of Latin style socialising and Frank and Daisy felt great for it. In no time at all, it was time for Gino to run them back to the Airport. They were upgraded to first class for the flight back to the UK., courtesy of Gino's friend who happened to be the co-pilot, it was just the Italian way of doing things: Gino always knew someone, no matter what needed doing.

Frank and Daisy breezed through baggage reclaim, collecting their "priority" baggage before completing passport control, at Gatwick. As they walked through into the arrival lounge, there was a limousine driver waiting, holding a sign with their name on it. He had been sent by Ben, who wanted to chip in and help as his siblings were already doing their bit to make the holiday work.

'This is just what I needed.' Frank murmured, contentedly, to his wife as they sped westwards. The plan had been to simply take a taxi but a limo, ready and waiting was a far better idea.

It was almost dark by the time they arrived back at Chestnut Cottage and the couple were too tired to inspect the results of Daryl's efforts. Sam had left the heating on low for the evening, he reckoned that his parents might be missing the Italian warmth and he had made sure that they had enough supplies for the next couple of days, before going back home when the builders finished for the day.

Early the next morning, they were both impatient to see the progress of their new building and were up with the lark. As Daisy went downstairs to make a cup of breakfast tea, Frank went to the front of the house to open the curtains.

Although he did not notice many things, the sight of the front garden, shocked even him. All the roses and young shrubs that they had planted along the edge looked as if they were dying, with yellow leaves and brown spindly flowers hanging limply. How was he going to break this news to his wife who had put up with so much already since they had moved to Whisperswood?

'Here's your tea, Frank.' She announced as she reached the top of the stairs.

'I'm afraid you had better come and have a look out of the front bedroom window.' He said, glumly.

Daisy felt her heart sink. She knew straight away, from the tone of his voice that there was another problem. She put the drinks down on a bedside table and went to join him at the front bedroom window.

'Oh no! Look at the garden! Who could have done such a thing?'

'I'll run the CCTV back and see what it shows.' He tried to comfort his distraught wife

For the moment, their desire to see the new extension was somewhat tempered following the dreadful discovery. Even so, a tour of inspection was the first thing to be done, they were almost getting used to unpleasant surprises.

Everything exceeded their expectations; the building was wonderful. They were blown away as they walked through the luxury bedroom and en-suite bathroom, both of which, overlooked the river. Daryl had suggested a mezzanine floor when he had first looked at the plans and he had offered to put it in at no extra cost in case they Didn't like it. Like it? They loved it! It was marvellous and set the Huge room off perfectly. The only thing left to do was the decorating. Outside, the roof was all but finished and they expected the roofers to be gone by tea-time that day.

Inspection completed, Jack sat down with another cup of tea and began trawling through the CCTV recordings on his computer. He discovered that the perpetrator of the crime had visited at 22:32 hours on the first night after they had left for Italy. It plainly showed the owner of the "Organic & Vegan Vegetable Co-operative", an irregular, deliverer of over-priced produce, to the Corbinnes. She brazenly, walked up and down by the picket fence at the front of Chestnut Cottage, spraying something over the garden, before disappearing from view, on foot, in the direction of the Corbinne's address.

'There's nothing for it, we'll have to ring the cops…For what that's worth.' Frank said. He was beaten. He knew that the law enforcement service would do nothing about the vandalism, they hadn't done anything to help him so far so why would anything change? But the criminal law, solicitor who they had retained, since the first incident of harassment, had advised them to record everything, so that if they ever decided to take legal action, they would have plenty of evidence.

The Bests wondered how they had ended up living among such a dreadful bunch of people who were so malicious. On the face of it, these individuals lived in a quintessential English village and seemed to have everything but scratch the surface and they were insecure, jealous bullies.

Ten days went by, before they had a visit from a disinterested policeman in answer to the "101" phone call about the vandalised front garden. He pointed out that it might have just died in the summer heat. Frank showed him the video of the vegetable delivery woman's nocturnal activities.

'Do you know who that person is? It looks like a woman.'

'Yes,' Frank told him. 'she delivers garden produce, or something, to the Corbinnes, down the road, every now and then. She has an old van with a company name painted on it.'

'How often do you mean by, "every now and then"?' The policeman asked, taking his note book out but not opening it.

Frank had to explain that the Corbinnes did not appear to have any money but, wanting to keep up appearances and advertise their green ideals, took deliveries of organic food from this odd woman, on the rare occasion that they had a bit of spare cash. He did not know her name though.

'Unfortunately, without a name, there isn't anything we can do. You can't prove she's spraying anything harmful on the garden.'

'Why can't you ask the Corbinnes for her name?' Frank asked, exasperated now.

'Well I can't really go involving half the population in solving the riddle of your dead plants, the Police Service is short of manpower, I'm afraid, sir. The best thing I can suggest is that you keep a diary of events. If anything else happens, be sure to let us know.' He put the unopened notebook back in his pocket, it was only a prop.

Frank realised that he was wasting his own time listening the copper's endless excuses for doing nothing. He decided to thank him for coming and get rid of him as quickly as possible, which was easy, because the copper had the same idea. As he left, Frank asked him: 'Do you believe in karma, officer?' The policeman didn't understand the question.

'Never mind.' *It's a bitch and comes to most of us.*

They decided that the only thing to do was re-plant the front garden but not until they got around to it. Once they had got the house back from the tradesmen, they would never really use the front garden, it was more for the benefit of people passing by. The passersby would just have to look at dead shrubs and plants for the time being.

Chapter eighteen

Life Goes On

Life at Chestnut Cottage was wonderful. Spring was in the air and all the new planting around the extension was coming to life after winter.

Another Christmas had been celebrated but this time, with enough space for the grandchildren to run around and play any game they chose, while the adults chatted over Christmas cake and dessert wine, in the spacious new living room.

Mathew and Alice had invited Frank and Daisy to join them for lunch at "The Duke's Head" for no reason other than, 'why not?' It was nice to catch up with them as a busy work schedule often meant that they were unavailable for social dates.

As usual, it was a mad rush to get out of the door to keep the rendezvous. They walked briskly, under the first warm sun of the year and with the exercise, were getting a bit too warm by the time they reached the village pond. The duck was still there, a regular feature, and today was joined by a pair of mute swans, preening in the sunshine. 'How lucky are we to live in such a beautiful place?' Daisy said, looking at the fowls on the pond. 'Even the grass smells good.'

Matt and Alice were waiting for them at the bar, when they entered the pub. 'Where have you been? We're a drink ahead already.'

Once the late arrivals had been served, the four of them moved to a table by the window. Alice explained that they had just, in the last hour, won a lucrative contract and were out to celebrate. 'I hope you haven't got anything planned for the afternoon, Daisy!'

Over an excellent steak, the lighthearted chatter continued, with all the news flowing from one couple to another. The new contract was supplying goods to The Prince of Wales's "Highgrove" shop. Of course, that called for a celebratory round of drinks from Frank.

The dessert menu arrived and they were all pouring over it, when Alice suddenly remembered something that she had heard the day before. 'I was in the village shop yesterday and it turns out that Joan has a problem with the Council planning Department!'

'No!' Frank could not help himself.

'Absolutely. Apparently, she built her garage without planning permission.' Frank sat, mouth open, as she spoke. 'Anyway, it's got to come down, she's furious. It's been up years; long before you moved here but someone knew and they have reported her.'

'Shall we talk about something else, a bit more lighthearted?'

'Of course, Daisy.' Alice did not want to upset her. 'It's just that everyone was talking about them ganging up against you and now the tables are turning. There are people who have lived here a lot longer than they have, who turned a blind eye when she had her builders in, so now there have been a few phone calls. The boot's on the other foot, so to speak.'

'Up the backside, hopefully.' Matt quipped.

With the meal finished, they all accepted the offer of coffee and liqueurs, as the younger couple were intent on celebrating. More laughter and chat and before they knew it, the landlord was wanting to close his establishment for the afternoon.

The four of them, left the pub together through the front door, passing the pond once more, heading towards Chestnut Cottage. Everyone had agreed that they should spend the rest of the afternoon together, at the Best's summer house by the river.

As they walked, they were confronted by Mr. Big Nose, who decided to stop his large, status symbol car, in the road and open the driver's door wide enough to block their way. Frank and Daisy did not want any confrontation but Mathew stepped to the front of the group and said, 'Come on, Big Nose, grow up and get out of the way. Shut your door.'

Big Nose, feeling brave inside his car, just looked at him and said nothing. He was wearing a ridiculous smile as if to say, 'What's the problem?'

Mathew, said firmly but calmly, 'I will tell you one more time and then it gets real.' He started towards the car door, his temper rising. How dare this arrogant bastard spoil their celebration afternoon?

Big Nose realised that he may be in for a pasting if he did not back down and he slammed the door shut, as they all trooped past him.

Frank put a hand on the other man's shoulder and said, 'Don't let him get to you, our chance will come.'

'He's just the sort of tosser I can't bear. You know, the type who always have to have a cardboard cup of coffee on the go, metrosexual, about as far from being a man as can be. You know what I mean, Frank. Like in your house, you do the "blue" jobs and Daisy does the "pink" jobs.

'That's Daryl's saying.' laughed Frank. 'He can't stand Big Nose's sort either.'

'Yes well, Big Nose does the pink jobs and pays a man to do the blue jobs' he laughed. 'Not many real men in Whisperswood.'

Daisy interrupted their conversation with, 'Come on, another coffee at ours.'

'Make it an Irish one, large!' Replied Alice. That made them all laugh. They raised a toast to the "begrudgers". 'May they all find some happiness in their life.'

The afternoon floated by, much like the fish they could see in the river as they sat and talked about everything from the first dragonfly of the year, to the latest political headline.

The sun finally started to sink in the west and the air began to cool. Mathew drained his drink, flopped back in his chair and declared: It's time we had a bit of a get together, all our friends in the village.

'So, shall we have a dinner party? After all, the whole story began with one!' Frank joked.

'Go on then,' Alice joined in, 'Who shall we have at the table and who is just going to be on the menu?'

Epilogue

Karma

So, there is the story: Daisy and Frank had legally applied for and achieved their planning permission; all above board but the price they paid, was high. They had bought a derelict cottage, virtually uninhabitable with no running water, overrun with rats, with an acre of land that hadn't see the light of day for the best part of a hundred year; a sad little house that no one had wanted.

They now had a very desirable, spacious home, with beautiful gardens and the most amazing views. A large garage and a lovely contemporary, family room, all that they needed for their extended family, had been added but at a cost.

Regrets, they had none. They were near their family and friends; it had worked well for them. The gang of bullies, having drawn a line in the sand, would now have to live with the consequences. It was amusing to watch the odd relationships develop.

Joan now appeared to be keeping a lower profile but she has found new victims to direct her hatred at. Her husband is home from the rigs and retired, so they are stuck with each other and can no longer 'turn the picture off'. She doesn't walk so well these days and as they both irritate each other; she lets him borrow a dog to walk, for the few hours that she is at home. That keeps them separate all day. No one knows, or cares, what they do at night, but Mr. Joan's garden shed has a pair of curtains at the window. Two of her dogs have died and she drags the surviving three, around the village as far as she can manage.

Mr. and Mrs. Big Nose are waiting for a divorce. Her father died and left nothing but debts. It was the final straw for Mr. Big Nose, he left her the next day and eloped to Swindon with the mysterious woman from the Garden party. Mrs. Big Nose, desperate for his return, still refuses to agree to grant his wish.

Joan fell out with Gail, once the lack of any inheritance came to light and they no longer speak. Her daughter, Tiffany, has left home and Gail has replaced her with cats, lots of cats. Daisy never understood why people do that, indeed, Frank's sister always had a house full of cats, but why? A cat is only interested in itself and they do say that people can be like their pets.

Mary Mac. still makes sticky jam to sell outside the house next door and sticks her nose in other people's lives. She still counts cars, hoping one day to see herself on the local television news as the savior of Whisperswood.

Moaning Mac has become a recluse and no one has seen him for a year. Someone got planning permission to convert the cow shed that he viewed as his cricket pavilion, into a bungalow. It now has a conservationist living in it, who insists on keeping the "cricket ground" as a natural meadow and the grass is about three feet high throughout the cricketing season. Moaning Mac. Had said: 'Over my dead body!' And it looks as if it probably will be!

The Rose's sons are all growing up into young men and one by one have left the cramped, crumbling hovel, to discover the delights of the 21st Century, such as running hot and cold water. One of them managed to get a grade 'F' in his geography GCSE. and he keeps his mother confined to her own garden and has confiscated all her cutting tools.

Mr. "Wandering-hands" Jones and his wife are now living in a local nursing home, where neither of them know who the other one is. Mr. Jones had a stroke and lost the power of speech. He constantly writes notes demanding a single room of his own as he does not like the woman he is sharing with because she won't stop talking. And he cannot tell her to shut up! He has no idea that the cause of his discomfort is his long-suffering wife.

In the next room to the Joneses, is Mrs. Lupus. She tripped over one of her Jack Russells whilst trying to stop one of Joan's dogs from digging a hole in her garden and broke her hip. She has been in a wheelchair ever since. Oh, to be a fly on the wall in that nursing home.

The cake lady moved to Spain, she really didn't belong in Whisperswood and finally found her vocation as a nun in Santiago de Compostela. Her husband, Justin, stayed on in the village for a while but soon had a terrible accident with his hired mini digger, when the throttle stuck and it ploughed through the kitchen wall and into the dining room, finally coming to rest against the opposite wall.

When he discovered that the house insurance had lapsed, he gave in and jumped on a ferry to Spain as well. He left his half-demolished house just as it was, the mini digger still embedded in the dining room wall. No one has ever seen him since, including the bank that holds the mortgage on the property. They had assumed that he would be joining his wife but he was bound for Magaluf to live his dream of being a nightclub DJ. He will never be found; his fake identity is of the highest quality and once his plastic surgery has healed, even his wife will not recognize him.

The lady who talks too much, who thinks that Grandmothers are "granny bores" and her husband who drinks too much, have been very kindly presented with a clutch of grandchildren. She discovered that she had the feelings for them that most women are born with and she finds them actually quite enjoyable. She never misses an opportunity to bore anyone she meets, with endless anecdotes about her funny little kids. Hopefully the next time she judges someone, she will give it more thought before she opens her mouth.

Frank and Daisy are now a younger version of Hugh and Ruby to Mathew and Alice. They remain great friends with Bunny and Eric and always meet up for a jar whenever the latter are over, from their foreign base. They enjoy a passing greeting with the other inhabitants of Whisperswood, most of whom, ignore Joan.

Frank continues to have eye problems but found that ground floor living transformed his life. With Daisy fussing over him, life is good.

It was rather unfortunate that they had come across such a nasty bunch of people. Frank remarked: 'Not everyone does the right thing in the right place at the right time and not everyone knows if they have got it right or wrong.

    Mr. And Mrs. Best are no longer the latest arrivals in Whisperswood, another cottage has changed hands since their battle against the bullies. The cycle continues: neighbours, good and bad, living side by side. Everyone starts out as the newcomer.

Printed in Dunstable, United Kingdom